PROTECT

DOMS OF CLUB EDEN, BOOK 4

L. K. SHAW

Protect, Doms of Club Eden Book 4
© 2017 by LK Shaw
Cover design © 2022 by PopKitty Design
All Rights Reserved.

No part of this book, with the exception of brief quotations for book reviews or critical articles, may be reproduced or transmitted in any form or by any means, electronic or mechanical, including photocopying, recording, or by any information storage and retrieval system without express written permission from the author.

This is a work of fiction. Names, characters, places, and incidents are the product of the author's imagination or are used fictitiously, and any resemblance to actual persons, living or dead, business establishments, events, or locales is entirely coincidental.

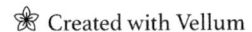

❦ Created with Vellum

CHAPTER 1

My name is Detective Daniel Webber, and I am in deep shit.

It all started a year ago when I was working on what I thought was an open-and-shut case involving a murdered prostitute. We had the john in custody, and he'd confessed. That was where I fucked up. I'd let a rookie cop make the arrest. A rookie cop who made one of the biggest mistakes a cop could ever make. He neglected to read the suspect his Miranda rights.

I wasn't diligent in my duties and a killer walked.

I was on the verge of being suspended so I made sure to tread lightly around other not so open-and-shut cases. One of which hadn't been opened yet when it was brought to my attention. A young boy was suspected of being abused by his uncle, who had become his guardian after the death of the boy's adoptive parents.

I was already on thin ice with my Chief, so I had to take care with unfounded presumptions. I couldn't start hounding a man without proof. This was where I fucked up again. The man who'd brought the allegations of abuse to me, Connor Black, was somewhat of a... frenemy, for lack of a better term. We weren't enemies, but we certainly weren't friends.

The boy had called his birth mother for help. I went to speak with her and instantly felt a spark of attraction. An attraction that became sort of a pissing contest between Black and me considering he was in love with her. I was so intent on pushing Black's buttons that I lost focus on what my end goal should have been: taking care of people in need.

I forgot I was a cop.

I forgot my job was to serve and protect.

A job I failed to do. Lives were almost lost, including that of Black's ladylove.

Then, a month ago, I was involved in yet another case, one that brought to light a significant amount of corruption within the department. Corruption in the higher echelons of the entire public service entity, starting with cops in my department, including the Chief, all the way up to the Mayor's office. I held all the evidence and shit had been going down ever since. People I trusted and respected were dirty. With the way I was feeling about the whole situation, it made me want to take justice into my own hands, especially when it involved the trafficking of women.

Because of my connection to the collector of said evidence, my career was in even further jeopardy and my life on a downward spiral. Losing myself in booze and women became my coping mechanism. Maybe it wasn't the best choice, but fuck it, it was how I dealt.

Today had been the longest day this week, and I was ready to head home and crack open a cold beer. Or three. Then *she* walked into the precinct. The most beautiful woman I'd ever seen even though she was covered head-to-toe in dirt, her shirt and pants torn in various places, and her dark brown hair a wild rat's nest atop her head. What struck me the most though, were her eyes. They were almost a piercing blue, like ice. And filled with fear.

Her breathing was shallow, and her glance darted hastily around the room as though searching for enemies in the shadows. Seeming to sense my stare, her eyes honed in on me. For several moments, neither of us broke eye contact. It seemed she was taking my measure, as I was hers. Instinctively, I knew that whatever brought her here would either be my downfall or my redemption.

I slowly made my way over, making sure when I reached her that I stayed out of her personal space. I knew if I invaded it too soon, she'd spook. And there was no way I was letting her out of my sight anytime soon.

"I'm Detective Webber. Is there something I can help you with?"

Her bottom lip quivered at my words as tears sprang to her eyes, but she gained control quickly, blinking them back.

"Is—is there some place private we can go?" She spoke so softly I had to strain to hear her.

I hesitated only briefly before inclining my head. "My office is this way."

I led the way to the back of the precinct, only glancing behind me once to see if she followed. I ushered her into my office and closed the door. She took a seat in the vacant chair on the near side of the desk.

I wanted to remain close, but also wanted to put her at ease, so I made my way to the other side and sat in my own chair as opposed to the seat next to her.

"May I get you something to drink?"

She shook her head. "No, thank you."

"Ok, how about we start with your name then."

She cleared her throat and let out a huff of air. "My name is Katherine Marsh."

Katherine. I savored the sound of her name inside my head.

"And, what can I help you with, Katherine?"

She looked down at her clenched fingers but remained silent.

"Katherine." I coaxingly spoke her name again, trying to gain her trust, but not push her. "Whatever it is, you can tell me."

She finally looked up at me, her lips bloodless and white. "I saw someone murdered tonight."

I tried to hold back my shock, although I wasn't sure how successful I was. "When did this murder take place? Where? Are you sure the victim is dead?"

Without thought, I pulled out the notepad I always kept with me from my inside coat pocket.

"I'd just finished my shift at La Scala, the Italian restaurant downtown, when I went out to the alley to take the trash to the dumpster. It was about 10:00 pm. I heard raised voices coming from farther down the alley. I thought I recognized one of them, so I headed in that direction. When I turned the corner, there were two men standing there arguing. I was about to announce my presence when one of the men reached out to the other man and pulled him close. At first, I thought I'd interrupted a lover's quarrel and that one man was embracing the other in an attempt to stop the argument. Until the second man stumbled and fell to his knees that is."

She paused in her speech and swallowed several times, hard. Tears again built in her eyes; this time, there was no stopping them as they raced down her dirt-stained cheeks.

"I stood there and watched the man topple over, holding his stomach, before I realized something was wrong. I knew I needed to move, but my feet were stuck. I must have made some type of noise, although I can't be sure, because the standing man began turning toward me; that's when my brain began working. I ducked out of sight behind the dumpster, held my breath, and prayed like I'd never prayed before. I heard movement and footsteps, but they sounded like they headed in the opposite direction. I waited another few minutes before peeking around the corner. The only thing I saw was the man lying on the ground. Before I could even think about what I was doing, I rushed over to check on him. He was dead."

She barely finished the last sentence before a ragged sob escaped. She covered her face and cried as though her entire world had just come crashing down. There was nothing I hated more than seeing a woman cry. I swiftly moved around my desk and knelt before her, touching her shoulder in comfort. I rocked backward, barely catching the both of us before we toppled over, as she threw her arms around me and wept into my chest. I held her for what seemed like hours, both of us on our knees on the floor, trying to ignore the press of her breasts against my chest.

Against my will, I felt myself harden as her luscious curves pressed against me. It was then I noticed the quiet. Her sobs had died down, and she was pushing herself closer to me. I pulled back slightly, causing our cheeks to glide against each other. Before I even knew what was happening, our lips met in a fierce kiss. Her mouth opened to the coaxing of my tongue, and I didn't waste another second. My tongue darted in and began to play with hers, tasting her. I withdrew my tongue and was about to plunder her mouth again, when she ripped herself out of my arms.

Katherine jumped to her feet, and with a hand over her mouth, a horrified expression across her face, she began backing away from me. She bumped into the door and quickly turned to flee the room. Her hand had just touched the doorknob when I finally came to my senses and clumsily stumbled to my feet. "Wait, Katherine. Don't leave. Please."

Like I said. Deep shit.

CHAPTER 2

Oh my god, what was wrong with me? Emmett had been killed before my eyes, and I was sitting here, making out with a cop. My behavior appalled me. I needed to focus on finding Emmett's murderer, not this sexy-as-sin cop. His California good looks—with his tanned skin, shaggy, sun-streaked brown hair, and forest green eyes were not a distraction I needed. The man who had treated me like his daughter was dead. And I was the only person who could bring his killer to justice.

The plea from the detective had me frozen, indecision warring inside me. I was embarrassed by my behavior, but the grief-stricken side of me wanted justice. Or vengeance. I didn't care which.

I turned back to Webber and really studied him. I noticed the ruddy cheeks, and it hit me that he was probably just as, if not more so, embarrassed as I was about what just happened.

"Please accept my apologies for my behavior. It was unprofessional and highly inappropriate."

"No, it was my fault. I'm sure you didn't realize you were going to have a hysterical woman on your hands. No reason for you to apologize. Let's just forget it happened. Okay?"

He hesitated only briefly before nodding.

"Please, have a seat. I need to ask you a few more questions if that's all right."

Both of us returned to our previous seats, the atmosphere now tense with awkwardness. I was also pretty sure I looked a mess, even without looking in the mirror. I knew from past experience that I was not a pretty crier. My skin turned blotchy, my nose bright red. Not that I cared how I looked. I wasn't trying to impress him.

He reached for his discarded notepad and pen. He cleared his throat once and swallowed hard before asking his first question.

"The man you found dead, did you know him? You said you thought you recognized one of the voices of the men arguing."

For a moment, grief almost consumed me again, but I maintained my composure. "His name is—was—Emmett Jackson. He owns La Scala, so he was my boss. He was also my surrogate father. I didn't recognize the man who stabbed him. After I realized Emmett was dead, I ran back to the restaurant and called the police. I didn't share my name, only telling them what I'd witnessed and where to find Emmett. The killer could be anyone. I don't know for sure that whoever was in that alley last night was actually gone. I was, and still am, scared, Detective."

His scrutiny during my explanation had my skin itching. "You say you're scared, but I also sense another emotion. Anger. You have the look of someone planning something. What if the killer saw you in the alley? What about some type of protective custody until we find him?"

I thought about it, but immediately discarded the idea. I could only pray that I hadn't been seen. I knew I wasn't going to hide, no matter how scared I was. After everything he'd done for me, I owed it to Emmett to bring his killer to justice.

"No protective custody. I plan on doing whatever needs to be done to find whoever did this."

"I hope you don't plan on doing anything reckless, like trying to find the killer yourself. You need to leave the investigating to the police."

"I told you I plan on doing whatever I have to do to bring Emmett's killer to justice."

I knew I was being stubborn, but I'd learned from the best. Emmett had been the most bullheaded man I knew. And the only father I had ever known. My heart was beyond broken.

"If that's the case, why even come to the police? You said you made an anonymous call. No one would know it was you. If you're so hell-bent on bringing a killer to justice, then why not just do it?"

I sighed in disgust. "Because I'm not completely

stupid. I came here in the hopes that someone would help me. You just happened to be the first person to approach me."

"If it's vengeance you're looking for, you came to the wrong place. There are laws in place for a reason. The world can't have vigilantes running around meting out their own justice. That is what the courts are for."

I could only stare at this person in front of me, who, fifteen minutes ago was the most attractive man I'd ever met. The heat from that kiss still burned inside me. But the person who kissed me with such passion seemed to have disappeared. Instead, he was replaced with someone who talked about laws and rules. I studied him further, gauging every word he'd just said. It hit me then that something about his tone didn't ring true.

"You said everything a by-the-books, emotionless cop would say, but why do I get the feeling that even you don't believe a word you just spoke? And who said anything about a vigilante? I want justice to be served. And I'll do whatever it takes to make sure it's done. Whatever it takes. The question is—are you going to help me or not?"

I sensed his frustration and indecision. I don't know why I was pushing so hard for his help. For some reason, my instinct told me that the only person who could help me was this man right here. I was essentially asking him to, if need be, break the law for me, and I realized I didn't even know his first name.

I interrupted his thoughts, because I needed to know his name. "What's your first name, anyway?"

He seemed startled by my question. "It's Daniel."

"I'm asking you again: Will you help me do whatever it takes? Please, Daniel?"

Instantly, I knew what his decision would be. Resignation flashed across his face, and I almost felt sorry I'd pushed so hard.

A sense of relief washed over me when he nodded. "Yes, I'll help you."

CHAPTER 3

After escorting Katherine out of the precinct with the promise to be in touch soon, I headed out to the alley to see if there was anything left. The crime scene investigation team on the case would have been thorough in gathering and processing all the evidence, but I needed to see everything for myself. I knew it was late and would be almost impossible to see anything, but it didn't matter. I couldn't explain it, but I'd always had a sixth sense when it came to solving cases. The fuck-ups happened when I ignored my instincts. It was eerie how I would often show up to a scene after the fact and get a vibe. It wasn't as though I could touch an object and see something. Nothing so voodoo hoodoo as that. Intuition perhaps? Regardless, I had it.

I found an on-street parking spot a block away from the upscale Italian restaurant. I made my way to the alley that ran behind the restaurant and walked in the direction Katherine had described earlier. The glare from my flashlight reflected off the puddles of what I prayed was water. A rat scurried through the beam of light shining across the alley before vanishing behind the dumpster. A shiver ran down me. I fucking hated rats.

I came to an abrupt halt when I spotted the large area of blood staining the concrete inside the crime scene tape that hung haphazardly from the light poles. Stooping under the tape, I slowly swept my flashlight back and forth, illuminating as much of the area as I could considering it was almost pitch-black out. The adjacent lights barely cast a dull glow. So far, nothing about the crime scene stood out for me. It was like any other. Continuing to look around for a bit and spotting nothing, I had almost given up when my "spidey-senses" started tingling.

I stepped over the bloodstain and began scanning the perimeter where trash and refuse lay. A sparkle shined as my flashlight beam landed on something. I bent down and fished a handkerchief out of my inside jacket pocket. Using the small piece of fabric, I picked up the glinting piece of metal from the ground. I stared at the bright, shiny, and extremely expensive looking cufflink. It was silver, the size of a nickel, except square in shape, and embossed with a black dagger. How apropos that the victim was stabbed to death, although I had no proof that this belonged to the killer. Anyone passing through this alley could have lost it. But something told me otherwise.

I wrapped up the piece of jewelry and stuck it in my

pocket. After another fifteen minutes, I knew I was out of luck and wouldn't find anything else that might lead me to the killer. I needed to figure out how I was going to run prints without going through the proper channels. Instinct told me I needed to stay under my Captain's radar. With any luck, I'd figure something out. In the meantime, I needed to head home for some sleep. I'd already worked a twelve-hour shift, and I'd spent another hour traipsing around here. I wouldn't be any good to Katherine if I was too exhausted to even focus.

∼

After catching a few hours of sleep, I spent the next hour debating on making a phone call or heading into the station to pass what I'd found to the detective on the case. I knew good and well I'd be out of a job if I kept this piece of evidence to myself. Yet, I didn't hesitate to continue going forward with what I was about to do. I pulled out my phone and tapped out a number I had no desire to call.

"Why are you calling me on a Saturday morning? Someone better be dying or I'm going to kick your ass the next time I see you. Which I hope isn't any time soon."

I swallowed the bitter pill in my mouth before I could speak. "Actually, someone is already dead. And I need a favor, Black."

Heavy silence filled the air. Finally, Black broke it. "What kind of favor?"

"I need you to swab a piece of evidence for DNA for me. See if you can find a match."

"I assume because you're asking me to do this, you're doing something that is going to be completely and utterly fucked up."

Three times now Connor Black had been a part of cases where things had gone south; it wasn't a surprise he thought I would fuck something else up. The fact that he focused on that and not on all the people I've helped and criminals I've put away in my fifteen years on the force stung. I was a good cop who joined the academy because I wanted to do right for my community. I'd never taken money to look the other way. I was honest and, if I had to brag, I was smart. I'd made a couple mistakes, and Black would never let me forget them.

"If I didn't need your expertise, I'd tell you to go fuck yourself. Now, are you going to continue to bust my balls or help me?"

"Fine, I'll meet you at my office in thirty minutes."

With the utter silence, I knew Black had disconnected the call.

I jumped into the car, and as I drove to Black's office, I thought about last night and my intense, and highly inappropriate, reaction to Katherine. What the hell had I been thinking kissing her like that? I was lucky she didn't file a complaint against me. I also thought about how I was going to handle her need to find the murderer. My conscience, which worked hard to be the kind of cop who followed the law and brought justice to those who needed it, warred with the man who would do anything, including breaking laws I fought to uphold, just to take the terrified look out of Katherine's eyes.

I pulled into the parking lot and stared at the building before me. It was now or never. I let myself in and took the five flights of stairs up to where I knew Black's office was located. His door stood open, and I could see him sitting behind his desk, reading glasses perched on his aquiline nose. I noisily cleared my throat just to see if I could get a rise out of him. Petty, sure, but I couldn't seem to control myself.

He looked up, seemingly not bothered by me in the least, and removed his glasses before setting them down on the desk. With annoying nonchalance, he sat back in his chair, propped his feet up, and placed his hands behind his head. A sense of déjà vu hit, only this time, our positions were reversed. I was now the one who needed help.

"You must be desperate if you've come to me. There must be a woman involved."

I tried to hide my shock. "What makes you think there's a woman?"

He chuckled and stared at me like I was an idiot. "We're not exactly bosom beaus. You're asking for my help at—" he glanced at his watch— "ten o'clock on a Saturday morning. There are few things in this world that reek of that much desperation, and a woman is at the top of the list. So, what can I do for you? And this woman?"

Considering he was right, I didn't want to waste time arguing. I pulled the baggie out of my pocket and placed it on the desk. "I need you to see if there is any DNA on this and run it if there is. See if you find a match in CODIS."

He reached out and began studying the object. "You said someone is dead. Is this the victim's or the killer's?"

"Honestly, I don't know. But if I had to take a guess, I'm going with killer. Someone witnessed a murder last night, and I found this at the crime scene. I need you to tell me who it belongs to."

"And by 'someone', I assume you mean a woman? Why aren't you going through your own channels to process this? Why come to me?"

I hesitated, not sure how much I was willing to share. Because honestly, I wasn't even ready to admit it to myself.

"Let's just say this one is off the books."

Black sighed in disgust. "Christ, it *is* a woman."

"Jesus, you're not going to let it go, are you? Yes, it's a woman. She came to the station last night saying she'd witnessed the murder. She's bound and determined to find the killer, because apparently, she knew the victim. I'm trying to keep her safe and out of trouble."

Black threw his head back in laughter and didn't stop, even when tears threatened to fall. What a dick. When he finally gained control of himself, still emitting a chuckle or two and wiping imaginary tears from his eyes, he looked over at me. I bit my tongue to hold back my words.

"Well, isn't this ironic? It looks like you've finally met your match, Webber. I can't wait for the show to start." He held up his hand when I started to speak. "Let me reach out to one of my contacts. He owes me. I'll just add it to your tab. Give me a couple days and I'll see what I can find for you."

CHAPTER 4

PATIENCE HAD NEVER BEEN one of my virtues. I wanted things to happen, and I wanted them to happen now. Emmett always laughed at how impatient I got. My current situation was no different. It had been close to twenty-four hours since I'd met with Dan—Detective Webber.

I was tired of waiting. I had already read a book, cleaned my apartment, and even run to the grocery. And I still hadn't heard from him. What was he waiting on? I had the day off and everyone from work had called me at least five times asking if I knew what had happened to Emmett. I didn't tell anyone what I'd seen. If I weren't hoping for Daniel to call, I would have turned my ringer off, because I was tired of fighting the tears when someone called. A knock at the door startled me. I ignored it, hoping the person on the other side would give up and go away when no one answered. The knock came again, this time accompanied by a loud voice.

"Katherine, you better be in there. Open the door."

What was Dan—damn it, Detective Webber—doing here? I thought he would just call me, not show up in person. It should have seemed odd that I recognized his voice, but it wasn't. I had no trouble recognizing his voice. His smell. His taste.

I picked my emotionally battered body up off the couch and went to open the door. "How did you know where I live?"

He walked past me into the apartment and immediately made himself at home at the dining room table. I followed, taking the seat next to him.

"I'm the police, Katherine. It wasn't that difficult to track down your name and address. I just went to La Scala and asked around. Your friends at work said you stopped answering the phone three hours ago. They were worried about you."

"So, what, they just gave some random man my address? Are they trying to get me killed? They don't know you from Adam. Maybe you were the one who killed Emmett?" I huffed in exasperation.

"For God's sake, Katherine, you're being melodramatic. I showed them my badge. It's not like I just went up to someone and asked for your information."

Melodramatic? He thought I was being melodramatic? "For your information, *Detective*, there is a killer out there. Yet you're not even the slightest bit concerned that my co-workers didn't hesitate in giving you my personal details? I'm a dead woman." I jumped up from my chair in disgust, but only made it two steps before he too stood and reached out to snatch my hand. He pulled me toward him, drawing me into his personal space. My breath caught as he reached out to sweep my hair off my face. He slowly closed the distance between us, giving me time to stop what I knew was about to happen. When I didn't, his lips softly touched mine. It was a brief kiss, but one I felt to my soul.

"No one will harm you, Katherine. I'll do everything in my power to protect you."

"Katie. My friends call me Katie." I could only whisper, almost stupidly, after his heartfelt words. Words that touched something deep inside me. No one but Emmett had ever given two shits about me. And now this man, Daniel, whom I had only met last night, was vowing to protect me. I didn't know what to think. But it felt good. Right. As though I was meant to be his to protect. To cherish. I shook my head at the crazy thoughts.

"Are we friends, Katie?" My name had never sounded so sexy rolling off someone's tongue. He softened the "t" sound, and his voice dropped an octave when he said it. A shiver raced through me, causing the tiny hairs at the back of my neck to stand and goosebumps to dot my arms.

"We could be," I practically purred. *What the hell? Was I flirting?* I needed to rein things in before they got out of hand. I cleared my throat and stepped out of his arms. "I mean, you said you'd help me find Emmett's killer. I guess that would make us friends."

He seemed to almost deflate at my words. As though he were disappointed in my retreat. Especially after that kiss. But my focus needed to remain on finding Emmett's killer. "So, what do we do first?"

"What do you mean?"

"I mean, what do we need to do to find Emmett's murderer?"

"First, *we* aren't doing anything. Second, I'm working on it. I went to the crime scene after you left my office last night and found something that might be a piece of evidence. Someone is taking a look at it for me, but until I hear back from him, there is nothing more to do but wait. I'm not the investigator on this case, so I have limited access to what was found at the scene before I arrived. Not unless you're willing to come forward as a witness. Otherwise, we're going to have to do this my way. My ass is the one on the line here."

I almost screamed in frustration at his words. I needed to help. To do something. It looked like I was going to have do this on my own. This was what happened when you tried to rely on people. My mother had taught me that.

"Fine, do what ever it is you need to do. But know this, Detective, so will I. Now, if you have nothing further, I'd like to go to bed."

We remained staring at each other, neither of us giving an inch. I couldn't help but gloat a little inside when he glanced away first and shook his head. Eventually, he'd come to realize how bullheaded I was and that I wasn't letting this go.

"Since I know I'm not going to change your mind, I'll be going. Just remember what I said about doing something stupid, Katie."

I escorted him to the door, a plan already forming in my head. "Thanks for stopping by, Detective. I really do appreciate any help you can offer."

Just as I was about to close the door behind him, he turned and reached into his pocket, pulling out something. "I want you to call me if you need anything. And I mean anything. I'm here for you."

He placed the object in my hand, closing my fingers around it before turning to walk down the hallway toward the elevator. I closed the door, opened my hand, and stared at the card with, what I guessed was, his personal cell number hand-written on it. I laid it on the counter before grabbing my purse and heading back out the door. I made my way to the stairs at the opposite end of the hallway where Daniel went and crept out the side door of the building, not noticing the man hidden in the shadows across the street, watching me.

CHAPTER 5

It didn't come as a shock to me when I saw Katie scurry out the side door of her building. She had pointedly ignored my statement about not doing anything reckless. It hadn't taken a genius to figure out that she was up to something. I just didn't know what. I watched as she walk-jogged across the street and hopped into a car. I jumped into mine and started following her when she pulled out.

When I realized she was heading downtown, I had a feeling I wasn't going to like where she was going. She parked two blocks from La Scala, and I quickly found another spot. I thanked god it was so late, otherwise I never would have found a parking place. I discreetly followed her as she darted around the corner. I had no idea what she thought she'd find at the crime scene that we hadn't already found.

Katie surprised me though. She bypassed the crime

scene and headed the next block over. I noticed a homeless man slumped against the wall whom she quietly approached. She bent down and gently shook his shoulder. He jerked awake and lashed out, causing her to jump back quickly. I started to intervene, but I saw that Katie had it under control when the man immediately relaxed when he saw her. His reaction seemed to indicate that he knew her.

She squatted down and started speaking to him, but I was too far away to make out what they said. Her shoulders slumped in disappointment when I saw the man shake his head. Whatever answer he gave her was not what she wanted to hear. I cleared my throat loudly, making my presence known. They both startled and whipped their heads in my direction, Katie emitting a small shriek of surprise. A look of distrust crossed the man's face, while irritation spread across hers.

"What the hell, Daniel? You can't go around scaring the crap out of people. And what are you doing here?"

A small smile escaped at the sound of my name on her lips. It was obviously a slip of the tongue that she didn't even realize she'd made.

"That's what you get for sneaking off like that. And to answer your question, I followed you. You were too agreeable back at your place. I knew you were planning something. Now, what are *you* doing here? And who's your friend?"

She sighed in resignation. "This is Skeeter. He lives

around here, and I was hoping maybe he saw something last night."

"From your expression, I'm guessing he didn't." It wasn't a question, even though she shook her head anyway.

"Nothing. Now, I'm back to square one."

"You mean, *we're* back to square one. Stop trying to get yourself killed. It's late, and you have no idea who might be out here. I understand your frustration, I do, but I can't protect you when you do reckless shit like this. I told you I would help you and I will. You need to be patient and trust me. Can you do that?"

She didn't speak for the longest time. I hated seeing her so disappointed, but I'd rather see her pissed off than dead.

"Fine. I'll be patient, but you need to promise me something. I need you to keep me in the loop. I've never been a patient person. If you find something, let me know. Don't keep it to yourself. I also need to feel useful. Emmett was like my father. I want his killer to pay."

I had already agreed to go against laws I'd fought so hard to uphold. I don't think she realized the lengths I would go for her. I knew it made no sense considering I only met her last night. I'd never believed in love at first sight before, until her. And maybe it wasn't love. But, if it wasn't, it was the closest thing to it. From the moment I saw her, all other women ceased to exist for me. It would only ever be her.

"I promise you, Katie. He will pay. Now, will you please go home? And at least try to stay out of trouble?"

Katie grudgingly said her farewells to Skeeter as I walked her back to her car. I followed her back to her place, telling myself it was just to make sure she reached home safely. I pulled into an on-street parking spot right behind her and walked her to the door. She stopped and turned so quickly I ran into her, almost knocking her over. I grasped her arms and pulled her against me to stop her from toppling to the ground. A small "oomph" escaped her full lips.

I couldn't help but inhale Katie's light scent. She smelled of vanilla with a hint of cinnamon. It reminded me of the spicy apple pies my gran made when I was growing up. Between the smell and the feel of this soft woman pressed against me, my mouth watered. Unconsciously, she moved against me, or maybe I moved against her, and I barely held back the groan that escaped, even as my cock hardened.

Her throat moved as she swallowed hard, and it was all I could do to not press kisses along her neck. I wanted to lick the spot behind her ear and see if she tasted as sweet as she smelled. Her pupils dilated, and her breathing became shallow. On top of her clean, fresh smell I was already craving, I scented her arousal. My cock swelled even further at the thought that she was as turned on as I was. The timing couldn't have been worse, and even though we'd just met, nothing in my whole life had felt as perfect as this. It was as though everything wrong in my life had been made right. I couldn't even begin to explain it.

Without thinking my plan through, I captured her lips in a bruising kiss. I swallowed her small gasp of surprise. Her body sagged against mine, and her hands came up to rest against my chest. My mind fought with my body about how wrong this was. Katie was witness to a crime I was, even if off-the-record, investigating. Her sighs of pleasure filled my ears, and my conscience wavered. Already I craved this woman, and knew I'd never get tired of tasting her.

I pulled back and rested my forehead against hers, our chests heaving from breathlessness.

"What have you done to me?" I pleaded for an answer. "You should be pushing me away, Katie."

Her finger plucked at my shirt. "I can't explain it either, Daniel. This explosion of emotion I keep feeling every time you're near is like nothing I've ever felt before. But, why do we need to question it? Why can't we just let it be whatever it is?"

I couldn't think when she was this close. My brain short-circuited, and my cock began making my decision for me. I stepped back and took a deep breath to try and regain control of my emotions.

"I'm a police officer, and you're a witness to a crime, Katie. I'm already walking a tightrope with my career and this—" my hands motioned back and forth between us— "could be what knocks me down and completely ruins everything I've been working toward since I entered the academy."

A look of hurt crossed Katie's face, my words cutting her deep. Then, her spine stiffened, and her expression hardened. She turned away from me to open her apartment door before turning back to glare at me. "I see. Well, thank you for seeing me home, *Detective*. I don't want to keep you from your important work. Go. Do what you need to do to make yourself feel better. Just remember your agreement to keep me in the loop with whatever you find. See you around, Webber."

Without another word, Katie closed the door in my face. I sighed in frustration. *Fuck*. I stood there a moment before the *snick* of the deadbolt sounded on the other side.

CHAPTER 6

I KNEW I was being unfair to Daniel, but I'd lost control of my emotions the minute I realized Emmett was dead. He had grounded me. When I was six years old, my mother disappeared for two weeks. She'd been on one of her benders and dropped off the face of the earth. It wasn't the first time I'd been left alone, but it was certainly the longest. I'd done my best to find myself food to eat, but we barely had anything to scrape by. After the second day without anything to eat, I'd been sitting on the front stoop crying in hunger, when the man who lived next door walked over and sat down next to me.

I'd seen him once in a while when I came home from school, but he kept to himself, except for those few times I'd heard him arguing with my mother about taking better care of me. He always smiled at me whenever I saw him. It was a smile that seemed sad and always made me want to do something to make him happy again. He never spoke directly to me, and I didn't know what his name was, but he seemed nice.

After sitting down, he introduced himself and asked me what was wrong. I was so lost, and even though my mother had always told me that our lives were no one's business, I was scared, hungry, and alone. An expression that had me scooting away from him in fear crossed his face when I told him I didn't know where my mother was, and I didn't have anything to eat. He quickly wiped the expression off his face, and I relaxed. He told me not to move and he'd be right back.

He disappeared in his house but returned a short time later. In his hands was a bowl of macaroni and cheese. Not really understanding that I shouldn't take food from strangers, I dug into the meal and quickly devoured it. Every day until my mother returned, I was invited to Emmett's house where he fed me and helped me get ready for school. Emmett was my refuge.

When I was old enough to understand, I asked him why he'd never called children's services on my mother every time she took off. He told me about how his wife and daughter had been killed in a car accident before I'd been born, and I reminded him of his own daughter if she'd lived. He said he knew that if children's services were called in, I'd most likely be sent to live in a foster home, and he'd heard too many horror stories about what happened to kids in foster care that he didn't want to subject me to that.

So, he did the best he could to take care of me and

made sure I had everything I needed. He was the one who helped me through the days I thought I was dying, when in reality, I'd only hit puberty. He went to my track meets and the father-daughter dance at school. He was at my graduation and co-signed the loan for me to buy my first car. He did everything a father should do for his daughter. There was no one I loved more than Emmett.

Just the thought of Emmett's body lying in that alley had me in tears again. I had to find his killer. I owed it to Emmett. My mind drifted back to Daniel, and I took a few minutes to examine my feelings. Things were so jumbled in my head; it was hard to make heads or tails of anything. One thing I did know though was that Daniel Webber had grabbed a hold of me in a way no man ever had before.

From what I'd learned about him in the short time I'd known him was that he had a strong sense of right and wrong. He saw things in black and white with minimal shades of gray. His dedication to his career and making sure justice was served was evident, but his rigid view of the world was skewed. Not everything was cut and dry. There were times when desperate measures needed to be taken. This was one of them.

Just knowing that somewhere out there was Emmett's killer had me raging against how unfair life was. Emmett had been there for me when no one else was. There was *nothing* I wouldn't do for him. I needed to try and get some rest tonight, because tomorrow, I planned on looking for Emmett's killer.

As I walked into La Scala, Emmett's restaurant, early the next morning, my eyes were gritty and my nose stuffy from crying all night. I'd barely slept from the nightmares. Emmett's body falling to the ground was playing on repeat throughout my mind, and I couldn't shut it off. I stepped through the door of the up-scale Italian restaurant and was assaulted with the familiar smells of garlic, basil, and tomatoes as well as the sounds of pots and pans clanging around in the kitchen as the staff prepped for the day. They were sounds and smells I'd grown up on as I'd been coming to work with Emmett since I was ten. My eyes teared up again, but I pushed the wetness away. Crying wouldn't bring Emmett back.

I headed back to the kitchen, weaving through the maze of square tables peppered throughout the restaurant, the white tablecloths bright and crisply pressed. It seemed like the world kept turning even though Emmett was no longer part of it. Clattering pots quieted when the staff saw me enter the room.

Erin, one of the sous chefs, rushed over. Everyone else resumed their duties, but I could tell they were all trying to eavesdrop.

"Oh my god, Katie, are you okay? I'm so sorry about Emmett. I can't believe he's dead."

When I didn't tear up, I realized I was all cried out. At least for now. There was no doubt that grief would continue to hound me at unexpected times.

"Thank you, Erin. I was just heading to Emmett's office. To take care of things, you know."

Erin only nodded. It wasn't strange for me to pop into his office and look things over. Emmett had been grooming me to take over the restaurant for the last two years. I'd been learning the ins and out of the business since Emmett decided to make me a partner not long ago, and I wanted to look over the books to see what I was going to need to keep things running now with Emmett gone.

In order to avoid going into more detail, I excused myself and moved through the kitchen back to Emmett's office. I closed the door behind me in hopes of avoiding any interruptions. My shoulders slumped the minute no one's eyes were on me. My gaze scanned the small office, stopping to look at various items scattered around, including the picture of me at my college graduation sitting on the edge of the desk. Emmett had been the proud papa that day. He'd invited everyone he knew to La Scala for a huge graduation party. The place had been packed. Everybody loved Emmett.

I plopped down in the chair behind the desk and took a few deep breaths, trying to gather my fortitude to dig into my least favorite aspect of the business. I hated math, and accounting gave me hives just thinking about it. Once I gauged I was as ready as I was going to get, I unlocked the desk drawer and pulled out the ledger. For two hours I read through every entry in that damned book until my eyes crossed. My brow creased and a headache had started behind my right eye. Something wasn't adding up. Emmett had only skimmed over the basics of his accounting so far, but he'd promised in the next few months he would sit down and let me take a closer look. I needed to take a mental break so I headed out to the kitchen before the lunch crowd started trickling in and grabbed a quick bite to eat. Then, I headed back in to the office.

Another thirty minutes looking over the numbers didn't make them any clearer. I needed to have them reviewed by an actual accountant. A sharp knock interrupted my thoughts, and I groaned in frustration. I needed to make it clearer next time that I wanted to be left alone. When I opened the door to the intrusion, I was surprised to see Daniel on the other side.

CHAPTER 7

My cock instantly hardened the minute I saw Katie's face. Everything about this woman turned me on, even though I knew she was trouble, and I needed to keep my dick in check. Her glare spoke volumes about what she thought of me popping in unannounced.

"What are you doing here?"

"I stopped in to ask some questions of the staff. I spoke with my Captain and asked to be put on the case. I'm not the lead detective, but he's letting me be a part of the investigation. I knew I needed access to the details if I was going to help you."

She appeared shocked at my statement. As though she was surprised I would go to such lengths, especially after our argument the night before. I had never been more serious as I was when I told her that nothing would harm her while I was around. Which meant I needed to be around. And getting involved in the investigation was the only way I could do that. Captain Peters seemed reluctant to let me in, but I'd been working hard on keeping my nose clean and earning back my reputation as a good cop. Although, for some reason, keeping the cufflink strictly between Connor and me seemed imperative. Just something my gut was telling me.

"I'm sorry I was so bitchy last night. I know you're trying to help."

"Don't give it another thought. I know how important finding Emmett's killer is to you. Do you mind if I take a look around?"

She shook her head, opened the door to let me in, and then closed it behind us. Probably not a good idea since I couldn't seem to keep my hands to myself when we were alone, but I refrained from saying anything. I needed to ignore this pull between us. Nothing more could happen. I'd already been playing with fire as it was. My focus needed to remain on finding the killer and making sure that, in the meantime, Katie was protected in case she'd been seen. So far, I'd been doing a piss-poor job of it. I'd left her alone two nights in a row. Anything could have happened during that time.

"What were you doing when I got here?"

"I was going over the ledgers and seeing what needed to be taken care of soon, like ordering food supplies, payroll, and other mind-numbing accounting things. But, I keep running across a mismatch of funds, and I can't figure out where it's coming from." A confused look appeared on Katie's face, as though finding an error was the last thing she'd expected.

"What kind of mismatch?"

"Well, there's a deduction of funds, but there isn't any note as to where they went. No vendor was listed, and even though the subtracted funds seem to be larger than the amount the restaurant brought in, the final sum still leaves the restaurant in the black. And this has been happening for several years. Up until a couple of months ago, at least. Then, suddenly, it stopped. According to the numbers I'm seeing, the restaurant should be in the red, but based on the bottom line shown, it's the exact opposite. The final numbers show a profit, but the math shows a major loss. In fact, I'm not even sure how La Scala is still open. It just doesn't make sense."

I walked over to where she'd moved as she explained the ledger numbers and now stood beside her. "May I?" I nodded at the books on the desk.

She pushed the book closer to me, and I picked it up to get a closer look. She leaned in until her shoulder brushed mine as she pointed at the numbers on the page. I froze at the contact. Her head turned slightly, and our eyes met. Her cheeks flushed, and she hastily took a step back. I scanned the page in front of me, making a note of the numbers she'd been referring to. I did some quick calculations in my head and realized she was right. Nothing was adding up.

"Do you have Emmett's banking information? Statements of any kind?"

Katie nodded and then started rummaging through a file cabinet against the wall. She pulled out a manila folder and handed it to me. It was filled with bank statements. I quickly flipped through a few of them. I couldn't make heads or tails out of any of this. The loud ringing of Katie's phone interrupted my concentration. She picked it up off the desk and swiped across the screen.

"Hello?"

Katie's face drained of color, and a terrified light entered her eyes, instantly putting me on high alert.

"What do you want?" Her voice came out shaky, and her whole body trembled.

Not caring about anything but finding out who was scaring the shit out of her, I grabbed the phone out of her hands.

"Who the fuck is this?" I barked at the unknown person on the other end of the line.

A deep chuckle sounded, which only fueled my anger.

"Well, hello, Detective Webber. It's nice of you to join the party."

My grip tightened on the phone so much that I wouldn't have been surprised if it snapped in half. "Don't make me ask you again. Who is this?"

"Don't take that tone with me, Detective. I can make your life extremely miserable if you piss me off. I recommend you show me a little more respect."

"Fuck you. I don't know who you are, and I don't give a shit. Don't threaten me again, because you have no idea how miserable I can make *your life*."

The silence was heavy after my outburst. Then, clapping broke the silence.

"Bravo. What a good show. You sounded just like a knight willing to put his life on the line for his damsel. I applaud your spirit. However, that lapse in showing me the proper regard will cost you. I'll be in touch soon."

A bellow of rage burst from deep inside me when the line went dead.

"Fuck." I checked myself when I almost threw Katie's phone against the opposing wall. Instead, I slapped it none too gently on the desk. Instantly, my gaze searched out Katie's. She remained pale, although some color had returned to her face. But, her whole body still shook with slight tremors. Without conscious thought, I pulled her into my embrace, holding her tight and trying to relieve her shaking. Eventually her chills eased, but she remained in my arms.

"What did he say to you?" I needed to know what had caused her initial reaction.

She spoke so softly I had to strain to hear her. "He said I was going to wind up like Emmett if I didn't give him what he wanted. You snatched the phone before he could tell me exactly what that was."

Damn it. Things had just escalated, especially with the threat to Katie. And the caller clearly knew who I was. I needed to talk to Connor and get some answers. In the meantime, I needed to keep Katie safe. Which meant keeping her close.

"You're coming home with me."

CHAPTER 8

Hearing that voice tell me he was going kill me, even if he hadn't used those exact words, had sent chills running through my body. I was scared shitless. I wanted to be pissed off that someone would threaten me, but nothing in my life prepared me for this. Even other cokeheads and my mom's drug dealer popping in and out of the house at all hours of the night when I was growing up hadn't left me as terrified as I was right now. In fact, I would normally balk at Daniel's, at anyone's, command, but right now, I didn't want to be alone.

What the hell kind of mess had Emmett gotten himself, and now me, into? I hadn't even realized I'd been shaking until Daniel had taken me in his arms. I grabbed onto him and held tight. Something about him soothed me. I felt more safe and protected with him than I had with even Emmett. After a few minutes, my tremors abated. I reluctantly pulled myself out of Daniel's embrace. I never realized how nice it was to lean on someone else. I'd had a few boyfriends over the years, but in actually, they were *boys*. Daniel was all man.

"All right." I could tell I'd stunned him with my easy acquiescence. It was understandable since I'd gone off half-cocked last night and headed back to the alley alone to talk to Skeeter. My mind finally comprehended how much danger I was in; it was clear now that whoever killed Emmett had seen me. Although, I didn't understand why he hadn't come after me in the alley that night. Maybe something else had scared him off. Or maybe he needed me for something. Either way, I was going to trust Daniel.

He shook off his surprise. "Okay. Let's finish up here. Bring the ledgers with you, so I can have them looked at by a friend of mine. Then, we're going to stop at your house, and you're going to pack whatever it is you think you'll need for the next week. I'll have someone drive your car back to your place."

I gathered up everything I thought was important, locked up the office, and said my goodbyes to the staff, letting them know I was going to take a few more days off. I let them know that Maurizio, one of the restaurant's managers, was in charge while I was gone, and if they needed anything, he'd get a hold of me.

Daniel led me out of the restaurant and out to the car. I waved distractedly to some of the lunch regulars who were starting to trickle in. We took off down the road with my eyes scanning in front of and behind us, trying to see if I could tell if any one was following us. I was suddenly extremely paranoid.

"Hey, are you doing okay?" A light touch landed on my thigh, and I looked down to see Daniel's hand.

My sob was disguised as a laugh. "I'm doing as well as I can be considering someone just threatened to kill me. Honestly, right now, I'm holding on by a thread. I'm pretty sure any second I'm gonna completely freak, out and then you're going to have a hysterical woman on your hands. You're going to have no idea what to do with me, and then you're going to freak out. Then things are going to get really bad, and I totally know I'm babbling right now, but I'm scared shitless. I'm trying to cope by talking and not thinking about what could possibly happen to me."

My mouth snapped closed, and I started breathing fast as though I was starting to hyperventilate. Black spots danced in my eyes, and my head was spinning. Abruptly, my breath was taken away in a different way when Daniel's mouth slammed down on mine. His fingers fisted in my hair and tugged slightly as he slanted my head to get better access to my mouth. Every thought left my brain when his tongue coaxed its way between my lips and tangled with mine. He tasted of mint and coffee, and I never wanted the kiss to end. I lost all track of time and space as the kiss went on.

I'd been kissed more times than I could count in my life, but every one of them before Daniel paled in comparison. He kissed me as though his life depended on it. He put his heart and soul into the kiss. At least, it felt that way. His teeth nipped at my bottom lip as he pulled away. I could feel my body leaning toward his as though chasing the kiss, not wanting it to end. Reluctantly, my eyes blinked open, and I stared at Daniel's face in front of mine. He looked as affected as I felt.

Now that I'd stopped my mini melt down, I realized Daniel had pulled off to the side of the road and removed his seat belt to get to me. I couldn't believe I'd been so panic ridden that I hadn't realized the car had stopped.

"You better now?" he asked cautiously, as though I was about to have another almost break down.

My breathlessness now resulted from his kiss and not my anxiety.

"I'm fine. Sorry about that. Everything just hit me at once."

"Totally understandable. You've had a stressful few days. I would be more worried if you weren't terrified."

Once he saw that I was back in control, he pulled back out on the road. A short time later, we pulled into my apartment complex. Daniel pulled into a spot and came around to my side just as I was stepping out of the car. I led us into my place.

"Go ahead and get your stuff."

I nodded and quickly headed into my room to get my things. I grabbed my duffel bag from the hall closet on the way and then stood at my closet, staring at my clothes. What did a person take with her when she was hiding out from a cold-blooded killer? Knowing that time was an issue, I just starting pulling clothes off hangers and shoving them in my bag. I'd barely left enough room for my crap from the bathroom, but I managed to shove some basic toiletries in there as well. After straining to get the thing zipped, I heaved it over my shoulder and strode back out to the living room where Daniel was just putting his phone back in his pocket. Although I was curious who he'd been speaking with, I didn't ask any questions.

"I'm ready."

CHAPTER 9

After I got Katie and her bag loaded in the car, we drove in silence to my house. I'd called Connor while she packed, and I was headed to his office after I dropped her off at my place. I hated to leave her alone while I met with Connor, especially since the caller knew who I was. Chances were he could easily find out where I lived, but I was betting on it taking him at least a day or two before he realized that Katie was no longer home. Which meant I needed to work fast to figure out who he was.

I pulled into the garage of my small, Cape Cod-style home in a suburban neighborhood equipped with its own neighborhood watch. It was actually the first home my parents had owned before they started having kids and had to upgrade to something a little bigger. It had gone on the market about six years ago and because of the condition of the house, it had sold at a far lower than market value price for the area. I spent two years, during any spare time I had, fixing it up. It wasn't big, but it was enough space for a bachelor or a newly married couple like my folks had been.

After grabbing Katie's bag, I helped her out of the car and into the house. I couldn't help but watch her facial expression as she took in my home. For reasons I didn't care to analyze, I wanted her to like the place.

"If you follow me, I'll show you to your room." Her footsteps sounded behind me as I walked down the hall to the guest bedroom across from mine. Knowing she would be sleeping only a few short feet from me had me twitchy. Katie was here for protection, nothing more. It seemed I was going to have to keep reminding myself of this important fact.

I set her bag on the bed as her eyes scanned the room. It wasn't anything fancy, just a double bed covered by a bright-checkered quilt my mother had made by hand, a chest of drawers, and a yellow fabric papasan chair in the corner.

"I know it's not much," I said, almost self-consciously.

"What? Oh, no, it's perfect. Thank you so much."

I nodded my head. "The bathroom is across the hall to the right, and my bedroom is to the left. There are towels under the sink and an unopened toothbrush in the drawer. I don't really cook, so the only thing you're going to find in the fridge is beer. I'll run to the store and pick up some things if you want to make me a list. I eat a lot of take-out, and my mom and sisters try to feed me on occasion."

"How long do you think I'll need to stay here?" Katie's arms were wrapped around herself, and she was rubbing them as though she were cold.

Even though I wanted to comfort her, I kept my distance. Every time I touched her, it seemed to lead to kissing, and I needed to keep my head clear. Especially since I didn't want to stop at just kissing.

"Until I find the person responsible for killing Emmett and threatening you, I can't take any chances with your life, Katie."

She nodded distractedly. I wondered what she was thinking about. Her life had been completely disrupted; I'm sure this wasn't easy for her. I cleared my throat.

"I hate to leave you here by yourself when you just got here, but I need to meet with my friend about these ledgers. I also need to see if he's gotten a hit on a possible piece of evidence I found at the scene the other night."

Katie waved off my concerns. "Go. Do what you need to do, especially if it is something that might help with the case. I'll be okay here. Truly."

I hesitated for a moment, but when she didn't say anything else, I strode out of the house and headed to Blacklight Securities.

∼

THIRTY MINUTES later I was back in a place I immensely disliked being. Being beholden to Connor Black was not high on my to-do list, yet here I was, again, for the second time in almost as many days. As I entered the reception area, I spotted Black's resident hacker slash computer analyst. The last time I'd seen Josephine Bishop she'd had a gun shoved up against her ribs. She looked decidedly better today.

"Ms. Bishop."

"Detective Webber. Good to see you. And please, I told you to call me Josie." I shifted the ledgers I'd been carrying to my other side as she reached out to shake my hand.

"How have you been doing?" Josie'd been searching for a half-sister she'd recently discovered she had.

"As well as can be expected. I still haven't found her, but I haven't given up hope."

"I'm sure if there is anyone that can find her, it's you."

"Thanks. Anyway, Connor is expecting you. He asked me to join you guys today. I hope that's all right."

"Of course. I know your skills with the computer. I'm sure I'll have to grovel to Black to borrow them."

Josie laughed lightly. "You know he likes pushing your buttons just to be a dick. Don't let him get to you. I, for one, am grateful to you. So, even if Connor is a jackass, I'll help any way I can."

I smiled in appreciation as we headed to Connor's office. As usual, he sat behind his desk, reading glasses perched on his nose. Josie took a seat on the loveseat next to the fully stocked bar while I took the chair in front of Connor's desk.

"So, it looks like things just escalated with your lady friend based on your call earlier."

Just thinking of the threats to Katie had my blood pressure skyrocketing and anger burning deep in my belly.

"That mother fucker threatened to kill her. I neither know, nor care, who he is. He's going down."

Connor face remained expressionless, but the vein throbbing in his forehead spoke of his anger. I knew how he felt about women being threatened. "You said the caller seemed to want something from her. Does your girlfriend have any ideas what it might be?"

I glared at him. "Her name is Katie, and she's not my girlfriend. No, she has no idea."

"I'll have Josie tap into her phone in case he calls her again. I do have some interesting news for you, though, regarding that piece of evidence you brought in. Have you ever heard of Francis O'Reilly?"

"Frankie O'Reilly, the loan shark?" Puzzlement sounded in my voice.

"One and the same. His print was found on that cufflink. I also heard he has a fondness for knives. You know, as a little extra incentive to pay up."

I scrubbed my hand across my forehead and down my face. "Shit. I wonder if that has anything to do with these ledgers from the restaurant Emmett Jackson owned." I slid the books I'd place on the desk toward Connor, who picked one up to flip through it slowly.

"Katie pointed out to me some transactions that don't

add up. I have Jackson's bank statements here, but haven't had time to look at them yet. Even if I had, I'm no accountant." This was what I was dreading. "I was hoping you could take a look at Jackson's financials for me. See if you can figure out where the discrepancies are coming from. I need to see if they have any connection to O'Reilly. Katie is staying with me until this is over. And I need it over quickly."

Black looked me over, assessing me. I barely kept myself from fidgeting under the scrutiny. Then his gaze turned to Josie, who'd been sitting silently absorbing our conversation.

"Josie, I need you to see what you can find out about these unexplained withdrawals that Mr. Jackson seemed to be making and why he was making. I also want to know where the money from the withdrawals was going since the numbers in the books don't add up. Also, please put a trace on all calls to Ms...?"

"Marsh. Katherine Marsh," I interjected.

"Ms. Marsh's phone," Black continued. "Just in case this son of a bitch calls and threatens her again. It might also be worthwhile to pay a short visit to our resident loan shark, O'Reilly. Get a feel for him. The cufflink points to him being our suspect, but it never hurts to keep our options open. Besides, you might take him by surprise when you drop in unannounced. I've heard he frequents the strip club Sizzle. And clearly, Webber, you have the protection detail down. Keep your eyes open and your zipper closed."

I rolled my eyes in irritation. God, Black was such an asshole. As if I needed the reminder to keep my dick in my pants. Although, based on my reactions to Katie, it probably didn't hurt to be told again.

I said my goodbyes, with Black letting me know he'd notify me when Josie found something. Considering her skills, I didn't expect it would take too long for her to locate where the money was going. I was anxious to get back to the house, reluctantly acknowledging that I couldn't wait to see Katie again. Just knowing she was there waiting for me had my heart skipping with excitement. I pushed the feeling aside. She was a witness to a crime and she was only staying with me until the murderer was apprehended. After that, we'd both go back to our regular lives and never see each other again. The thought sent a sharp pang running through me.

CHAPTER 10

ONCE DANIEL LEFT, I began unpacking my meager belongings. Since I was going to be here for a while, I might as well make myself at home. My stomach growled, so I wandered into the kitchen and opened cupboards, looking for a snack. Holy shit, he hadn't been kidding when he said that he had nothing to eat. I found some stale saltines and a couple condiment packs of ketchup and soy sauce. There were a couple frozen dinners and in the fridge, a tub of butter and sure enough, practically enough beer for a kegger. Other than that, nothing. How did the man survive on practically nothing but alcohol?

I'd only been here for forty minutes and already I was feeling antsy. I knew Daniel was doing the best he could to find Emmett's killer, but I just needed to do *something*. The more idle I was, the more my mind kept returning to that phone call. That was the one place I didn't want to go. So, in order to keep myself busy, I did the only thing I could think of. I started cleaning.

Not that Daniel's house was dirty, but after growing up in a house that had fallen into disrepair due to neglect—drug addicts didn't pay a whole lot of attention to a clean house—I'd become obsessively compulsive about a spotless house. No used needles scattered around that a young girl could accidentally find. No half-empty cardboard pizza boxes and liquor bottles littered the floor. I dusted, vacuumed, wiped down kitchen and bathroom counters, cleaned the bathtubs, and took the trash out to a large bin I found in the garage. I knew it was excessive, but it was one of my many weird quirks.

I'd just finished taking a shower and had sat down on the couch to read for a little bit when door opened and Daniel walked in carrying a brown paper grocery bag. Suddenly, I was self-conscious about making myself so comfortable. His eyes darted around, scanning both the living room and kitchen through the open floor plan, taking the cleanliness in. Instead of anger, a twinkle of amusement lit up his eyes.

"I know I'm not the best housekeeper, but I didn't think I was that bad. Something tells me I could probably eat off the kitchen floor and not have to worry a bit about germs."

He closed the door and made his way to the kitchen, placing the bag on the island that separated the two rooms. My cheeks heated. "Sorry if I overstepped; I needed something to keep me occupied."

"No worries on that account. You're welcome to clean any time you want, although it's definitely not necessary. Regardless, don't think anything of it. I know I kind of left you to your own devices. If I could have avoided it, I would have."

"I know."

Daniel began pulling groceries out of the bag. A loaf of fresh bread was laid on the counter, followed by a box of noodles and a jar of spaghetti sauce. Milk, meatballs, a bag of lettuce, veggies, and a bottle of salad dressing went into the fridge. Lastly, a couple bottles of white wine went next to the items on the counter.

"It's not much, but spaghetti and meatballs are about the only thing I can cook and not fuck up. I figured a side salad and some bread would go with it."

"No, that's fine, thank you. I know having me here is a terrible inconvenience."

"You'd never be an inconvenience, Katie."

I dipped my head in embarrassment at Daniel's words.

"Anyway," he coughed, returning his attention to the groceries as though realizing what he'd just implied. "I'm glad you made yourself at home. I want you to be comfortable here."

"Thank you. So, what did your friend have to say? Did you find out anything?"

Daniel appeared reluctant to share the information with me. I wasn't having it though. "Spill."

He sighed in resignation. "I identified the owner of a

print on something I found near the crime scene. But I have no idea how long the item had been there, and it could belong to anyone."

"But you're pretty sure it doesn't." It wasn't a question.

"I can't say for sure, but, yes, my gut tells me it belongs to our killer. I plan on questioning him, off the record, of course, in the next day or so to see if I might be able to find anything out. You will have a tap on your phone that will run a trace on any calls you receive, so if our mystery caller decides to call again, we can attempt to locate him that way. A friend of mine is having one of his techies comb through Jackson's financials to see if she can trace where all of his money was going, because it obviously, based on the numbers we saw, wasn't going back into the restaurant."

"Wow, your friends are awfully industrious. And definitely not a part of the police force, are they? You're taking chances with your career, aren't you?"

He shrugged. "Don't worry about me, Katie. I'm still a detective on the case. I'm just getting a little extra assistance from someone who's been known to help on occasion. As long as the case gets solved, it doesn't matter how it's done."

I studied him for a few minutes, our gazes locked, neither of us breaking eye contact. I could tell Daniel wasn't being entirely truthful, but there was nothing I could do if he was willing to put his career on the line. Especially after I'd begged him to do whatever he had to do to help me. A rush of guilt flowed through me at the thought that this man could lose a career he clearly loved because I'd asked for his help. He and I both knew it was vengeance and not justice I was truly seeking. I knew it was selfish of me, but I had a feeling we'd both gone too far to turn back now.

~

Daniel disappeared into his office after our brief conversation, and I settled on the couch, attempting to concentrate on the book I'd been reading. After thirty minutes, I gave up and went to my room for a short nap. I'd barely slept the night before, and utter exhaustion had me quickly falling asleep. When I woke up, it was dusk, and it took me a moment to orient myself and remember I wasn't in my own bed. I also felt more tired than when I'd lain down, but I forced myself to get up. Especially with the smells wafting through the door.

I walked across the hall to the bathroom and splashed some water on my face to try and freshen up a little. Then I headed down the hall toward the soft music playing and the delicious aroma that reminded me of Emmett. I stopped just short of the kitchen when I spotted Daniel. I smiled a little at the frazzled expression on his face as he spilled some of the noodles out of the colander into the sink. My smile grew when he cursed under his breath.

"Do you need some help over there?" I couldn't help the small bark of laughter.

He turned to glare at me. "Ha ha. Aren't you the funny

one? No, thank you. I am perfectly capable of making this damn meal." He paused for a long second before continuing. "I think. Have a seat and let me concentrate."

Daniel was adorable when flustered, but I didn't want to cause any more trouble than I already had so I followed his instructions and took a seat at the bar stool on the living room side of the kitchen island. His muscles flexed and rippled with each movement as he reached for different ingredients, causing my belly to flutter. He'd rolled his sleeves up, and I admired the tattoos I could see peeking out beneath. I wondered how far up they went and what the designs were.

"Is the salad ready? I can wash the lettuce and cut up the veggies if you need me to. You don't have to do all of this for me."

"Nope. You just sit and relax." He looked over at me. "You deserve to be taken care of."

Daniel turned around and went back to the meal prep before I could think of a response. My entire body melted at his words. This man was making me fall for him.

CHAPTER 11

IT WAS good hearing Katie's laughter. I had a feeling that life had dealt her a shitty hand, but she was tough. Her being in my house felt strangely right. I'd checked in on her earlier when she hadn't responded to my soft knock on her door. When I'd quietly opened the door and saw she was asleep, I'd watched her for a few minutes. The fear and worry that had been on her face the last couple of days had disappeared. She'd looked so young lying there, except her lush body spoke differently. Feeling like a creeper for staring at her unaware, I quickly shut the door and headed back to my office to get some work done.

After an hour, my stomach had growled; since I wanted to have dinner ready for Katie when she woke up, I shut down my computer and headed to the kitchen. That had been thirty minutes ago. Katie now sat at the island looking beautiful but still exhausted. I didn't know if nightmares were plaguing her sleep, but I knew she was suffering over the loss of Jackson. I made a mental note to go see O'Reilly tomorrow. See what he had to say about his missing jewelry. I was hoping my surprise visit would catch him off guard and he'd let something slip. I highly doubted it since O'Reilly hadn't made it as high up the crime ladder as he had by being twitchy.

"Tell me about yourself." I shot the question over my shoulder as I poured the sauce in the pan with the noodles and meatballs. I planned on letting it simmer for a little bit while I finished putting together the rest of our meal.

"There's not really much to tell." I heard the hesitancy in her voice as though reluctant to share anything personal with me.

"You said Emmett was like a surrogate father to you. What happened to your dad?" The only explanation I had for pushing her was that I wanted to know everything about her. It didn't help that as a detective, I was naturally curious.

I stopped what I was doing and looked at her. She fidgeted uncomfortably in her chair. Just when I was about to tell her to forget about it, she spoke.

"I have no idea who my biological father is. I doubt my mom did either. My mom died of a drug overdose when I was seventeen. She was never really around when I was growing up anyway; she was constantly chasing after her next high. Emmett mostly raised me. Or at least was always there for me."

"I'm sorry, Katie. I didn't mean to bring up bad memories."

She shook off my concern. "It was a long time ago."

I walked around the island and took her hand as I sat on the chair next to her. My other hand went to her chin and turned her face so she was now looking at me. Shame shone from her eyes.

"That doesn't mean it doesn't still hurt."

We stared into each other's eyes; mine were filled with sympathy for the young girl who'd lost her mother to the terrible disease of drug addiction. As a cop, I'd seen what drug addiction did to families, and I hated that Katie had grown up that way.

I'd just leaned forward, unable to stop from kissing her, when a hissing sound from the direction of the stove had me jumping back.

"Shit." I released her and hurriedly removed the pan from the stovetop as sauce bubbled over the edge and sizzled against the burner. *Damn it, I needed to focus on not ruining dinner.*

Once the pan was removed and the burner was turned off, I finished preparing our meal in silence.

"If you don't mind grabbing some plates out of that cabinet, I'd appreciate it." Katie followed my gesture to a cabinet next to the fridge. She set them next to me. "Have a seat at the table and I'll bring everything over."

"Are you sure I can't help?"

I shooed her off, and as she sat, I plated our food. I dished out the salad, set everything on the table, and then joined Katie. As we ate, our conversation steered clear of anything related to the case. I talked about my sisters and all my nieces and nephews. Food and wine flowed throughout the evening. I tried to ignore how nice it was to have a home-cooked meal with a beautiful woman across from me. I could easily get used to it.

Halfway through the meal I opened the second bottle of wine and refilled our empty glasses. Finally, we finished eating, and I rose to clear off the table. Katie followed me back to the kitchen and took her place at the island, sipping on her wine.

"Why aren't you married, Daniel?" Her words sounded slightly slurred. I made a mental note not to refill her glass again. I'd had my fair share of the wine so I was feeling a little buzzed as well. I finished loading the dishwasher, added the soap, and hit start before I turned around to look at her. Her elbow was propped on the island, and she'd rested her chin in the palm of her hand looking far too relaxed. And beautiful. She studied me in a way that had me hot beneath my collar.

"My career has been my life for the last fifteen years. I've busted my ass to get where am I. I work long hours, and it's not the safest job. It's hard dating someone when you may have to cancel at the last minute because of getting called out to a case. Or who you may only see for short periods of time because your work schedules conflict. Finding a woman who is willing to put up with that for the long haul is even more difficult."

Her nose crinkled in the most adorable way. "Well, that's just stupid. I mean, if she loved you, she'd understand how much your job means to you, how important it is, and she would just try to make the most of the time you do have together. I know I would."

Damn it, this woman was going to bring me to my knees. Every muscle in my body tightened as I resisted the urge to cross the room and take her in my arms. Something must have come through in my expression, because I watched as Katie suddenly set her wine glass on the counter and rose from her seat. She circled around to my side of the kitchen until she stood toe to toe with me. I flinched when her fingertips touched my arm, and she traced a path up to where my tribal tattoo peeked out from beneath my sleeve.

Her fingers danced across my skin, lingering slightly in certain places, as though not sure if she should proceed. I was frozen with indecision as well. Nothing good would come of this, but I couldn't seem to stop myself from letting it happen. When she sensed I wasn't going to stop her, she continued her exploration. Her palm cupped my cheek, and a giggle escaped her, as if the bristles of my unshaved face tickled her skin. My fists clenched with the need to reach out and touch her.

Her index finger traced my lips, and on impulse, I tasted it with my tongue. A shudder ran through her. The sensation pushed me over the edge, and I could no longer resist touching her in return. My hand reached out to lightly grab her wrist. I clasped her hand as I licked her finger. My tongue flicked it a few times before I sucked the whole finger in my mouth. It glistened with wetness when I slowly removed it. A whole silent conversation flowed between us as we stared into each other's eyes. Every interaction since we'd first met had been leading straight to this moment. We both knew it. It was time to stop fighting and let it happen, no matter how wrong it was.

In one fluid movement, I bent slightly and, with my hands under her ass, picked Katie up, forcing her to wrap her legs around my waist. Her arms instinctively went around my neck as our lips collided, tongues dueling for control. Only by luck did I back her out of the kitchen, her whole body plastered to mine, and through the rest of the house until we arrived at my bedroom. Moonlight filtered through the blinds, and I didn't even bother to turn a light on as we both collapsed onto the bed, never breaking our kiss.

I put every emotion I was feeling into the kiss. Even if I couldn't say the words, I wanted Katie to know how much I cared about her. She was everything I ever wanted. Hating to break our connection, I reluctantly pulled back. Her wet lips shone in the moonlight, and her hair laid spread out over my pillow, a backdrop of glorious silk I wanted to run my fingers through. My hands skimmed down her sides until I reached the bottom of her shirt.

I slowly tugged on the material, sliding it up her frame until her breasts were exposed. Katie leaned up as I pulled it up and over her head, tossing it aside. Then, she raised her hips as I removed her pants. Plain pink cotton underwear, that shouldn't have been sexy, but was, covered her sex. Needing her naked, I quickly divested her of those as well. My heart stuttered when I saw her bare pussy already slick with wetness. I licked my lips in anticipation of her flavor. Without removing my eyes from her body, I hastily disrobed, haphazardly dropping my clothes next to hers on the floor beside us.

I quickly returned my mouth to hers as both our hands began roaming and learning each other's bodies. Hers was soft and smooth in complete contrast to the hard planes of mine. I could spend eternity touching her and learn something new about her each time. I knew I would never tire of hearing the little sighs and moans she made.

One of my hands traveled the length of her side until I made it to my intended destination. Her breast fit perfectly in my palm. I lightly squeezed and caressed it, the tip hardening under my expert touch. Katie pushed her breast further into my hand, begging for more.

"God, yes, Daniel. Like that."

I loved when a woman told me what she enjoyed. I wanted to know all the ways to please Katie. What set her on fire. Where her most erogenous zones were. I wanted to learn them all. I drew small circles around the rigid nipple before sucking it into my mouth. My tongue followed suit, and I drew patterns around the tip before lightly biting down on it with my teeth. Katie's back arched, and a small scream escaped. Her fingers clutched my head, pulling me closer to her as she moaned out her pleasure. Every sound Katie made was like a song to my ears. I wanted nothing more than to please her, but the realization of finally being inside her was more than I could handle at the moment.

"I need you, Katie. I don't think I can wait."

"Make love to me, Daniel. I'm yours."

I reached into the nightstand then clumsily ripped open the condom wrapper before shakily rolling it down my length. I jerked when Katie reached out to surround my cock with her small hand. She directed me to her heat and placed me directly at her opening. Without waiting another second, I plunged my throbbing cock deep inside her.

Katie's fingernails dug into my back as I began to fuck her with everything I had. My entire body screamed in ecstasy at finally being inside her. The reality was so much better than any fantasy I could ever have.

I pulled one of her knees up to change the angle of my thrusts.

"You feel so good inside me, Daniel. God, touch me, please."

That was all the instruction I needed, and I moved my hand from her knee and reached down to rub her clit in a coordinated dance as I continued thrusting. Her pussy squeezed my cock, causing a groan to escape me. The muscles in her body tightened, and I knew her orgasm was seconds away. Increasing the pressure on her clit, I quickened my thrusts as my balls drew up. I was about to explode, but she needed to come first. My prayers were answered when her pussy contracted against my dick, and the orgasm rushed through her.

Katie's head was thrown back, and she screamed my name with the force of it. At the same time, my cock erupted as her pussy continued to milk every last drop of my seed. When the final tremor ceased, I pulled out of her and quickly disposed of the condom. For a brief moment, I wish it had lasted longer. My cock twitched with the need to be inside her again. Instead, I settled back on the bed and pulled her body close to mine, kissing her on the forehead. She wrapped herself around me and closed her eyes. Within moments, I knew she was asleep as her entire body relaxed and a small sigh left her lips.

"You regret it already, don't you?"

I turned my head from where I'd rested it on my linked fingers while I stared at the ceiling, thinking about all the mistakes I'd made in my career. I looked into Katie's eyes and saw her fear. I unlinked my fingers and pulled her closer to me. I kissed the top of her head.

"I thought I would. I mean, I should regret it. You're a key witness in a murder investigation, Katie." I couldn't help but sigh. "But, no, I don't regret it. I don't know where this leaves us, but I'm willing to see it through to the end."

Her fingers traced random patterns over my chest and then followed the lines of my tattoos before she began to play with the barbell through my left nipple.

"Who says it has to end?" Her voice came out soft and unsure.

"Oh, Katie. You don't want to waste your life on someone like me."

She quickly moved to an upright position and stared down at me, not caring or paying attention to the fact that the sheet pooled at her waist giving me a full view of her glorious breasts.

"Don't patronize me, Daniel. What gives you the right to decide what's best for me? The last time I checked, I was a grown woman who was fully capable of making her own decisions."

"I didn't say you weren't."

"Yes, you did. Maybe I don't think you're a waste of my life. Maybe I think you could be one of the best things to ever happen to me. Did you ever think of that?"

During her tirade, Katie'd jumped out of bed and begun gathering up her clothes that had landed around the room. She balled the clothes up in front of her as though using them for a defensive shield.

"I'm not afraid to go after what I want, but I'm also not going to push myself on someone who isn't interested.

Don't hang your insecurities on me, Daniel. I hope your beer keeps you company when you get old."

I remained silent as Katie walked out the bedroom door. I heard hers slam behind her across the hall, the echo of it mocking me in the darkness.

CHAPTER 12

Sleep eluded me after I walked out on Daniel. I'd felt closer to him than anyone else in my life, and he had to go and be a damn man and ruin shit. After tossing and turning for forty-five minutes, I'd given up on sleep. I needed some fresh air, and I figured a walk would do me some good. Help me clear my head. I threw my clothes back on and my sneakers and headed out into the neighborhood.

The sun had barely come up over the horizon, and I basked in the beauty of the purples, reds, yellows, and oranges in the sky. I couldn't remember the last time I'd seen such a gorgeous sight. You didn't get these kinds of views in the city. I'd been walking about ten minutes and had turned back toward Daniel's house. I knew I had to face him again, but I wasn't looking forward to it.

Every touch last night had been filled with care. Not just about pleasure, but with true feeling. There was something between us. Something strong, magnetic, and not to be ignored. I didn't know if it was something that would stand the test of time, but it was certainly something powerful and worthy of further exploration. And I knew I wasn't the only one who felt it.

I was so lost in my musings that I didn't hear the sound of a door opening or the footsteps behind me until a sack was thrown over my head and rough hands wrapped around me, trapping my arms against my sides. I screamed and kicked as I was dragged backward and unceremoniously thrown inside the running vehicle. Tires squealed and I was thrown against the wall; hitting my head so hard I saw stars.

When the dizziness subsided, I ripped off the bag and gulped in deep, cleansing breaths to get rid of the stale air inside my lungs. I was in the back of a windowless van. I leapt from the floor toward the door and had just grabbed the handle when another searing pain shot through my head as someone grabbed a fistful of my hair and yanked me back down to the floor. The muzzle of a gun appeared before my eyes, and all the blood drained from my face as I backpedaled away from it.

"Don't try that again, bitch."

I slumped against the wall, my eyes never wavering from the man or the gun in his hand. Slowly, he turned and settled back into the front passenger seat of the van. I studied his profile. He was bulky, all shoulders and no neck, with wet-looking black hair slicked back with too much gel. He wasn't fat, but completely solid. He reeked of Polo cologne and was clearly hired muscle. He had a bulbous nose, long forehead, and a wicked scar ran down the left side of his face. He had "don't fuck with me" stamped across his entire body.

From my position I couldn't see anything of the driver except the back of his head. There was no rear view mirror for me to catch a reflection. I absently rubbed my still smarting head and desperately tried not to think of what the hell was going to happen to me. My only thought was that whoever wanted me, must want me alive. At least for now. Otherwise, these goons would have just popped me as I walked down the sidewalk and left me for dead.

Instantly, my thoughts went to Daniel. I prayed he would find me and that my last words to him wouldn't be ones of anger. I prayed like I'd never prayed before. I estimated we had driven about forty minutes when the van slowed. From my vantage point, I couldn't see out the front window. Eventually, a shadow fell over the front window as we pulled into a building, and I could see the metal rafters of what looked like the inside of a warehouse. Finally, the van came to a stop.

The front doors opened and both men stepped out. Light spilled into the interior of the van when the side door was pulled open. "Scar-face", who again had his gun pointed at me as though I was going to make a run for it, stood in the open doorway.

"Get out." His gruff voice echoed in the air.

Slowly and gingerly, I crept out of the vehicle until I

now stood beside it. The warehouse went dark, except for some dim overhead lights, when the driver, I assumed, closed the large metal door of the building, shutting out the outside world and freedom. *Fuck.* Scar-face gestured with the gun for me to move, so I started walking across the cement floor. I kept moving, him right on my heels, toward an open door on the far side of the building where, inside the room beyond, a deep voice grew louder.

Hesitantly, I entered the room and caught sight of a good-looking older man in a sharp, expensive looking pinstripe business suit sitting behind a desk, talking on the phone. He had short dark hair with flecks of gray, black eyes, dark prominent brows, a strong jawline, and protruding cheekbones. He gestured for me to have a seat in the lone chair against the opposing wall.

My eyes scanned the bare room. Besides the man's desk and chair and the chair I was currently in, no other furnishings graced the room. The walls were bare. The room was clearly meant to be intimidating in its utilitarian simplicity.

"I expect we won't have any more problems," he spoke into the phone, a distinct warning evident in his tone, before ending the call without warning.

His dark, soulless eyes scanned me from head to toe, and I forced myself not to shudder while the fear poured through me. At that exact moment, it hit me: this man killed Emmett. I had no idea how I knew, but I did. In front of me sat his murderer. My mind raced back to that single phone call, and there wasn't a shadow of doubt that, whoever this person was, he would kill me too if I didn't give him what he wanted.

"Ms. Marsh. Emmett spoke so highly of you that it's nice to finally meet you." His conciliatory manner terrified me more than rage would have.

"I wish I could say the same." Inwardly, I cringed at my words. Sarcasm was a built-in defense mechanism I clearly didn't know how to shut off.

A burst of laughter came from the still unidentified man seated so deceptively casual in his chair. "Ballsy. I like it. Be warned, though. I only tolerate so much insolence, so I'd be cautious with the rest of my words, if I were you. Now then, I'm sure you're wondering who I am and why I've so graciously requested your presence here today." He didn't wait for a response before he went on. "My name is Francis O'Reilly."

He paused as though I should recognize his name. When he didn't get the response he so clearly desired, he scowled, but continued. "You see, your friend Emmett owed me money. A lot of money. And since he's no longer available to pay up, I'm forced to go to the next best place. You."

CHAPTER 13

After Katie stormed out, I continued lying there, battling with myself over whether or not I should go after her. After a few minutes, I figured it would be best to leave her alone. I didn't know what else to say to her anyway. It wasn't that I didn't care about her, because I did. Far more than I should. It was as though I was subconsciously sabotaging what could be a great thing, because I knew she was too good for me. My life was out of control, and she deserved more. She deserved to have to the best of everything, even if that meant having it with someone other than me.

Katie was amazing. She was kind, generous, and when she loved, she loved with everything. I could tell by how she spoke of Jackson. She was risking her life trying to bring his killer to justice. She loved him that much. What I wouldn't give to be loved like that. If only I weren't so stupid as to push her away. Even if it was for her own good.

After lying there for thirty minutes, I jumped in the shower to give her more time to cool off. I took my time getting ready, but finally, I knew it was time to face her. I needed to hurry up and solve this case before I made her hate me even more. As I stepped out of my room, I thought I'd hear her moving around, but a thick silence filled the air.

"Katie?" I called out. I turned back to knock on her door in case she'd fallen back asleep. When she didn't answer, I quietly opened it and peeked in. Her bed was unmade and empty. Taking stock of each room, I continued to come up empty. Katie was gone. *Son of a bitch.* Where would she have gone at this time of the morning? It was barely past dawn. Quickly, I threw on some shoes and headed outside. I hadn't even made it a block when Mrs. Beatty, one of the members of the Neighborhood Watch, who was practically pulling her dog behind her as she rushed somewhere, stopped me.

"Detective Webber, thank goodness you're here. I just saw some woman dragged off in a van. I was about to call the police. You have to do something."

"Shit. What did the woman look like? I need you to tell me everything you saw."

"The woman was a petite brunette with long hair. Extremely pretty. There were two men, big and bulky. I watch TV; I know hired thugs when I see them. One of the men threw a sack over the woman's head and shoved her in the back of a white van while the other man jumped in the driver's seat."

"Did you get a plate number?"

She appeared affronted that I even had the gall to ask her that. "Of course I got it."

I memorized the license number she gave me, thanked her, and ran back to the house. Fuck the department. I needed Blacklight Securities and Josie Bishop's hacking skills. Going through the proper channels would take far too long. I needed to find Katie now.

Dialing Black's number, I grabbed my car keys off the counter. Just as I dove into the driver's seat, I heard the click of someone picking up.

I didn't even give him time to speak. "They took Katie."

I threw the car in reverse, and tires squealed as I backed out of the garage and peeled away from the house to head downtown.

"How long ago?" Black's tone was all business.

"Within the last twenty minutes. We had a fight, and while I was in the shower, she must have decided to go for a walk to cool off. Goddamn it. I didn't think O'Reilly would find her this soon. One of the neighbors saw it happen. I need you to run this plate number on a white van, and have Josie check the traffic cams for anything."

I rattled off the license number as I headed toward town. I knew a few of O'Reilly's hangouts, and I didn't have time to waste. My gut told me if I found O'Reilly, I'd find Katie.

"I'll call you when I have something." With that pronouncement, he hung up. Black never wasted words.

What would normally take me close to forty minutes, only took me twenty as I pulled in front of a pawnshop on Mercy Street. One of O'Reilly's lackey fences worked there, and it was the best place I could think of to start. I reached under the car seat and pulled out my Ruger SR22. I stuck it inside the waistband of my pants at the small of my back.

The bell jingled as I opened the door. I didn't wait for anyone to come greet me, making my way around the counter and pushing aside the cheap ass curtain that separated the back room from the front.

I pulled out my gun as I stepped down the short hallway that opened up into the small storage room. I took quick stock of the place, noting the door against the opposite wall. I noticed a second door, but based on the lay out of the building, I knew that one was an exit to the outside. I had just reached for the handle when the door opened from the inside. Not giving Jonesy a chance to react, I slammed the door all the way open and barged in, gun lowered to my side, my eyes scanning the room for any immediate threats.

"What the hell, man? You can't be in here." Jonesy was a squirrely little bastard. He was short, thin, and wiry. His dirty blond hair was shoulder length and stringy, and his gold tooth gleamed when he spoke.

Not caring how many laws I was breaking, I grabbed him by the shirt and shoved my gun in his face.

"Where's O'Reilly?"

His eyes widened, and he threw up his arms in surrender.

"Yo, man, you don't need the gun."

When I saw Jonesy was the only occupant of the room, I pushed him around and slammed him face-first into the large wooden table, covered in pawned items and several piles of money, behind him. My gun went to the back of his head. I had no intention of shooting him, but he didn't know that. Jonesy was all about self-preservation, and I knew it wouldn't take much for him to start talking.

"Whoa, hey, now, you don't need to be so rough. I'll tell you whatever it is you need to know. C'mon, man, put the gun away." His arms were splayed out above his head, and his hands shook in a placating motion.

Needing to show him how serious I was, I shoved the muzzle a little deeper into his neck. "Don't make me ask you again. Where. Is. O'Reilly?"

"Okay, okay, the last I heard he was down in the warehouse district. That's all I know, I swear."

The ringing of my phone sounded overly loud in my ears. Keeping my gun trained on Jonesy, I reached for the device and swiped the screen.

"Tell me what you got."

"She's on Division Street. About three blocks down from Eden. I'll meet you there in ten."

He hung up, and I pocketed my phone and moved away from the cowering man sprawled out in front of me.

"If you warn him I'm coming, I'll be back for you. Don't fuck with me, Jonesy."

Without another word, I ran out to the car and raced toward Eden, a BDSM club I knew Black frequented with his wife. I'd been there a time or two when I was investigating abuse allegations Black had brought to me.

I'd just pulled into the parking lot across from Eden when Black arrived. He raised the back door of the SUV and, after pulling up the floorboard, grabbed several firearms and a wicked looking knife he stuffed down into his boot.

"Lead the way."

We jogged down the street until we reached the warehouse Black indicated. There were windows along each wall of the building, but none of them at eye level.

"Josie, I need you to see if you can get a look inside the warehouse. Hack into any security system O'Reilly has. I need eyes in there."

When I turned to Black, I finally noticed the Bluetooth receiver in his ear. Until we could see what was happening inside, we couldn't risk storming in there and endangering Katie. It was killing me not knowing if she was hurt, or even still alive. One thing I did know: O'Reilly was dead if he'd harmed her in any way.

CHAPTER 14

"Me?" I asked, slack-jawed. "But I don't have any money."

Shit. I was definitely a dead woman if this guy, O'Reilly, thought he was going to get money out of me. Especially if it was the kind of money you killed someone over. Which was something I needed confirmed.

"Were you the one who killed Emmett? I mean, if he owed you the kind of money you're saying he owed you, then why kill him? You'd never collect it with him dead."

He smiled in a way that made the hairs stand on the back of my neck. I shivered despite the heat in the building.

"I'd wondered if you saw me. I caught a glimpse of you when you dove behind the dumpster, but I wasn't sure how much you'd seen. Here's the thing about your friend Emmett." He sneered the name. "He refused to pay me what he owed me. He was also going to rat me out to the Feds about some things he had no business discussing. Things that could have cost me a lot more money."

"That still has nothing to do with me. I told you; I don't have any money."

O'Reilly laughed, a sinister sound that curdled the contents of my stomach. It was a menacing and terrifying noise, because he clearly knew something I didn't.

"Jackson didn't tell you, did he?" His words confirmed my thoughts. "Sweetheart, you have a lot of money. In fact, you're an extremely rich woman. You see, Emmett had a life insurance policy worth over a million dollars. And you are his sole beneficiary. So, Jackson's debt now becomes yours. With interest."

"How do you know how much his life insurance policy was for? Or that he left it to me? I'm sure that's not something he would just tell you."

"It pays to know people, Ms. Marsh. It also pays to discover everything I can about my investments. I invested in La Scala when it first opened. It was going to be the next Rao's of New York. Each year, Jackson began to slowly lose money. He borrowed money from me to put back in the restaurant, but soon, he wasn't able to pay me back. The losses have grown, and within the next two months, the restaurant was about to go belly up. Oh, dear," O'Reilly mocked, "you didn't know that either? What a shame."

I sat in mystified horror at what O'Reilly was telling

me. I thought back to the ledgers and everything made sense. The unexplained withdrawals with no known destination. The books showing a profit when, in fact, the restaurant was about to be shut down. But, why hadn't Emmett told me? How could he have done this to me? No, I shook off that thought. Emmett loved me and would never intentionally do anything to hurt me. He must not have known that O'Reilly would seek me out. If he was trying to put O'Reilly away, then he was trying to protect me. Something he'd been doing since I was six years old.

I continued in stunned silence as I processed everything. I was furious with Emmett even though it didn't do me any good. He was dead. All because of this greedy bastard in front of me. I knew Emmett had done what he thought best, and there was no way that he'd had any idea that O'Reilly would come after me. If there was one thing I had to believe, it was that. Emmett loved me too much to put a target on my back.

"Fine. The money is yours; I don't need it. Take it all."

O'Reilly seemed surprised by this. He must have expected more of a fight. And maybe I should fight harder, but now that I'd found Daniel, I had something to live for. Giving up the money was nothing if it would get this guy to leave me alone. I still wanted him to pay for Emmett's death, but I had to survive to do that. If that meant handing over whatever money I needed to, I'd do it. I'd find some other way to get justice served.

"Sadly, that's not going to cut it, Ms. Marsh."

My spine stiffened. I hated the way he said my name. It was condescending and patronizing.

"What do you mean? You just said Emmett left me over a million dollars. I'm handing it to you on a silver platter. You're getting your money. What else could you possibly want from me?"

O'Reilly rose from behind the desk and, like a snake, slithered his way over to my side. He propped one butt cheek on the corner of the desk and rested one forearm across his knee as he stared at me. I knew I wasn't going to like what he had to say next.

"Here's the thing, Ms. Marsh. I can't leave any loose strings untied. And you, my dear, are a loose string. As is your Detective Webber. You now know things that could cause me some serious problems. I don't deal well with problems. You see, I'm a fixer. If I see something I don't like, I fix it. Or rather, I have some of my associates fix it. You met them earlier today. Tony and Ricco. The first problem I plan on getting fixed is that boyfriend of yours. Do you know that I dislike cops immensely?"

He didn't wait for a response to the clearly rhetorical question. "Once I get my money, I'll be taking care of both you and your detective. Tidying things up and all. No hard feelings, you know."

Terror had taken residence inside me during his speech. The money didn't matter. Not in the end anyway. I could give him twice as much money and he was still going to kill me. And Daniel. This was all my fault. If I hadn't been so selfish as to want more than he could give me, we wouldn't be in this mess. No, I couldn't be satisfied with what he'd offered. I always had to have more. Now we were both going to pay. *Oh, Daniel. I'm so sorry I never got to tell you I love you.*

CHAPTER 15

My anxiety was through the roof while I waited for Josie to contact Connor. I needed to be in there. Even though we couldn't have been sitting here longer than ten minutes, time had slowed to a crawl, and it felt like hours. Sweat trickled down my back, and my trigger finger itched. I had no desire to kill anyone, but I would do what needed to be done to protect Katie. When I didn't think I could take it any longer, Connor spoke again.

"Talk to me, Josie."

I couldn't hear what was being said on her end, but Connor's replies were "yes" and "got it".

He looked at me and gestured toward the building. "There are three men, O'Reilly and two of his henchmen, and your woman inside. The men are hanging out in the main warehouse, and Katie and O'Reilly are in an interior office. There isn't any sound inside, so Josie can't hear what's being said, but based on the expression on your girlfriend's face, things aren't looking good. O'Reilly doesn't have a visible weapon, but the other two are packing. We're going to have to wait for them to leave."

"Goddamn it, Black, I can't just sit here and do nothing. What if it was Bridget in there?"

"Do you want to get her killed? Because that's what's going to happen if you go busting in there without a plan. I get it, Webber. I do. But you're too close to this. You're thinking with your emotions and not your brain right now. You know I'm right. We have to sit tight."

"Fuck." I knew he was right, but it didn't make me happy. At least we had eyes inside, and if it looked like things were going south, I was going in no matter what. Someone must have been looking out for me, because suddenly Connor straightened to attention.

"There's movement inside. Josie says it looks like they're leaving. O'Reilly just put Katie in the backseat of a Caddy, and got in next to her."

A metallic screech reverberated in my ear, and I jumped back as the large garage door to our right started opening. We quickly moved out of sight as the black car began pulling out. We watched as Tweedle Dee moved the car forward far enough for Tweedle Dum to close and lock the warehouse door behind him. Then, he hopped into the passenger seat and the car took off down the road.

"Josie, don't lose that car." Black's command was stern. I knew that she'd hacked into the traffic cams and would track the car from Blacklight Securities. Once the car was out of sight, Black and I took off at a run back to our cars.

"Get in," he hollered at me. I didn't hesitate as I quickly got into the passenger seat of his Escalade. He pulled out and turned left onto Division Street. I could only assume Josie was giving him directions on the other end of the phone.

Black and I looked at each other when my own phone started ringing. "Unknown" showed on the caller ID.

"This is Webber."

A voice I instantly recognized was on the other end. "Detective Webber, so nice to speak with you again. I expect you'll be a little more courteous this time around."

I needed to play this smart, so I couldn't let on that I now knew, not only his name, but also his every move.

"What do you want?"

I could hear Black say something to Josie next to me, but it was too low for me to make out.

"I have something that belongs to you."

"Explain yourself."

"Here, someone wants to speak with you."

There was a rustling sound as he passed off the phone. Even before hearing her voice, I knew who would be on the other end. I flinched nonetheless when Katie spoke in my ear.

"Daniel, please, don't listen to him. He's going to kill us both anyway."

"Katie, I'm coming for you."

"No, Dan—" The rest of her sentence was cut off as O'Reilly snatched the phone back from her.

"Now, you're going to do exactly as I say. You will come to this address, alone, I might add. You will not call any of your police friends. You will also come unarmed. I'd hate for any accidents to happen." He gave me an address on the other side of town. "You have fifteen minutes."

Katie's yell abruptly silenced when O'Reilly disconnected the call. I roared in frustration. I belted out the address to Black who immediately revved the engine, and the SUV surged forward as it sped up. Damn O'Reilly. He'd barely given me enough time to get to the location, which of course, was his entire plan.

"You know this is a suicide mission, right?"

"Well, let's hope you don't let that happen. Besides, he can try to kill me, but I won't go down without a fight. And Black, if he does manage to kill me, you get Katie out of there. No matter what you have to do, you get her out of there."

He nodded as he continued racing against time. Nothing mattered but Katie. Sooner than I expected, we closed in on the house. Quickly, Black got out of the driver's seat, and I took his place. He'd hoof it the rest of the way. I had to trust that he'd be there when I needed him.

I slowly pulled up to the palatial house of Mr. Francis O'Reilly. The gated entrance opened upon my arrival, and as I drove through, I scanned the grounds, looking for any signs of guards. O'Reilly seemed pretty confident since I didn't spot anybody roaming around monitoring the area. Either that, or they were good at hiding.

I drove around the circular brick drive and stopped at the front of the house. I hid my gun and the keys under the front seat and made my way up the walk, my eyes continuously peeled for signs of danger. I didn't bother knocking.

Slowly, I opened the front door and entered the giant foyer with sunlight streaming down onto the floor through the skylight above. The sun's rays bounced off the glass chandelier hanging from the vaulted ceiling, creating a myriad of colors and sparkles to dance across the walls.

Footsteps echoed through the air until there stood O'Reilly in his dark pinstriped suit that probably cost more than a month of my salary. I knew his reputation and knew he'd been brought in several times for questioning by other officers, but this was the first time I'd ever seen him in person.

"Welcome, Detective Webber. So glad you could join us. I trust you followed my instructions."

"Yes, I'm here alone. Now, where's Katie?"

"You know, there's one thing I've noticed today; during all this time, you've never once asked me my name. I don't believe we've ever met before today, so I'm wondering how it is that you seem to already know who I am."

I wasn't sure how much of my hand to show. My mind

raced with reasons why I shouldn't tell him. When I couldn't think of any, I explained.

"I found a cufflink at the crime scene where Jackson was killed. It didn't take me long to discover it belonged to you. I put two and two together. Well, there was also the money that Jackson was paying you every month. Or at least the money he was paying you until a couple months ago." *Check*. That last part was a total guess on my part, but it made too much sense not to be true. Why else would a high-class "money lender" kill someone? Because he was clearly not paying up. A dead or alive "client" didn't make a difference if O'Reilly wasn't getting his money. Somehow, though, he thought he could get it out of Katie. I just hadn't figured out how yet.

"Ah." He actually sounded impressed. "You must have some extremely intelligent and resourceful friends if you were able to find out all that information. But, you see, I also have smart and enterprising friends. They didn't seem to know anything about this piece of evidence you say belongs to me. In fact, I was told explicitly that there was nothing found at the scene to connect me to it. And as far as money goes, there is nothing illegal about someone paying back a friendly loan."

I shrugged nonchalantly. "I guess you need better friends."

O'Reilly chuckled loudly, his white teeth gleaming. "Perhaps you're right." He quickly sobered. "I'm going to need that cufflink back."

"Well, then we have a problem, because it is no longer in my possession." I paused. "However, I can get it with a simple phone call. All you need to do is hand over Katie. Then, it's yours."

Anger flashed across his face, marring his handsome features. "That's not how this works. You give me my property or your precious Katie is a dead woman."

"That's where you're wrong. You see, I might just be some dumb cop to you, but I have extremely well-connected friends. I also have a couple of friends in a little organization called the FBI. You see, Mr. O'Reilly, I'm not an amateur, and your cufflink, along with the evidence of payoffs made to you by Mr. Jackson that suddenly stopped not long before his death, is enough to prod my highly "resourceful" friends to dig a little deeper into your businesses. Something I'm sure you'll find quite inconvenient." *And, mate.*

Both of us knew I'd backed him between a rock and a hard place. Even if we made it out of here alive today, O'Reilly would be gunning for us. No one got the best of him and lived to tell about it. One day, he would get his revenge. It wouldn't be today, but I was now on his list of people whose life he would do everything in his power to destroy. He would strike when I least expected it. Insurance or not, eventually the cufflink and any other evidence I had wouldn't matter to him, because he hadn't built this empire by not greasing the right palms. Eventually, he'd find a way to recover everything, and then Katie and I would be dead. O'Reilly had a reputation of never forgetting slights, and this was the biggest slight of them all.

CHAPTER 16

Shortly after his alluding to the fact that he was going to kill Daniel and me regardless, O'Reilly had Ricco, aka Scar-face, escort me upstairs to a bedroom I would have normally swooned over. A king-size bed dominated the room, although it was housed behind two white floor-to-ceiling colonnades. The white and lavender duvet cover made the room appear bigger. A large soft gray settee stood at the foot of the bed, nestled evenly between the colonnades. A scrolled writing desk stood off to the side with a luxurious cushioned armchair of the same color as the settee tucked underneath it. Silver colored nightstands stood on each side of the headboard with glass stemmed lamps resting on top. The lines of the room were clean and modern.

When I'd walked into the en suite bath, I almost fell over. An in-ground bathing pool was housed in the middle of the floor, lights glowing from under the water.

White, fluffy towels were neatly placed inside cubbies on the white shelved walls. Silver fixtures shined beneath the track lighting. I felt like I'd stepped into a resort. Only reality intruded and reminded me that this was currently my prison. A high-class and elegant one, but a prison all the same.

I'd been warned that the windows were charged with a small volt of electricity, and should I try to open them, I'd be in for some unpleasantness. How many people had O'Reilly held prisoner here that he needed to zap them should they try to escape? I shuddered to think. It's possible he could have been bluffing, but he didn't strike me as the type of man who needed to bluff.

That had been forty minutes ago. I'd long since stopped pacing; and instead, I sat perched on the settee and bit my nails. It was a habit I'd kicked years ago, but with the stress of the day and worrying about Daniel, I'd unconsciously started chewing. It had always been a habit of boredom more than anything. When the snick of the door opening sounded, I sprung to attention, ready for anything.

When the figure behind the door stepped through, my heart jumped in my chest and began pounding a rapid staccato I could feel in my ears.

"Oh my god, Daniel, what are you doing here? I told you not to come? Are you okay?" I rattled off the questions as my hands and eyes scanned his body, checking for any injuries.

He grabbed my hands and lifted them to his lips to

place a soft kiss on them. "I'm fine, I promise. C'mon, we're leaving."

Daniel clasped one of my hands with his and led me out of the room and down the hall to the stairs. I didn't question him now, but followed the command in his hold. I was as anxious as he appeared to be to get out of here. We'd made it halfway down the stairs when O'Reilly stepped out of the office I'd left a short time ago. Anger was etched in his face, and every muscle in his body was tense. Whatever had transpired between Daniel and O'Reilly had him furious. Hatred spewed from his eyes as we silently walked past him. Neither Daniel nor I made eye contact. We just kept walking, Daniel's head held high and confident. We'd just reached the front door when O'Reilly's voice sounded behind us.

"I'll be seeing you soon, Detective Webber. You can count on it."

∼

WE'D BEEN BACK at Daniel's house for five minutes when the doorbell rang. I startled with nervousness; however, Daniel nonchalantly went to open the door. In stepped the biggest man I think I'd ever seen. He was a powerhouse, and it oozed from his pores. He was well over six feet tall, at least a couple inches taller than Daniel. He wasn't handsome in the classical sense, but something about him drew my attention. He emoted this air of control that had me slightly uncomfortable.

Immediately behind him walked in a couple. The man was attractive, with short brown hair that was graying at the temples and a slight amount of scruff covered his jaw. He wasn't overly muscular, but built more like a swimmer. He carried a large black duffel bag. The woman beside him was adorable in a girl-next-door kind of way with blonde hair cut in a bob and royal blue glasses perched on her nose. Beneath one of her arms was a laptop.

"Sorry I had to leave you behind, but I figured you could fend for yourself." Daniel addressed the giant.

"Don't worry about it. I'd already called for back up after you dropped me off so Miles and Josie were right behind us." He gave me a pointed look. "I think you should introduce us to your lady friend. She seems a tad twitchy."

Mildly affronted at the description, I forced my muscles to relax. Clearly, these people weren't a threat to Daniel or me.

"Katie, this is Connor Black, Josephine Bishop, and her fiancé, Miles Standish. Connor owns Blacklight Securities and has been helping me find Jackson's murderer."

I gave them each a small, uncomfortable wave and smile, and they all nodded in return. I didn't really know what to say to them. The woman, Josephine, made her way over to the dining room table and opened up her laptop. Her fingers flew across the keyboard, and a series of beeps could be heard until finally, she seemed to finish with whatever it was she'd been typing out.

"Your friend O'Reilly is calling in favors. Lots and lots of favors. I expect in the next day or two a contract will be out on your lives. You, Ms. Marsh, just cost one of the most powerful criminals in Pinegrove millions of dollars."

My head spun with this woman's words. Contract? Millions of dollars? This wasn't my life. It had to be a nightmare that I couldn't wake up from. None of this could be real.

"We're going to have to shut him down quickly. Because if anyone is going to die, it's not going to be Katie. I'll kill O'Reilly myself first." Daniel's impassioned words should have horrified me, but instead, I absorbed them, knowing that this man had proven over and over again that he would do anything to protect me.

Connor spoke up. "Let's hope it doesn't come to that. Josie has been looking into all of O'Reilly's business, both legal and not, trying to find something to put him away for life. Jackson isn't the first person he's killed. He just hasn't been caught before. Sadly, other than that small scrap of metal you found at the crime scene, nothing can put O'Reilly there. And that's circumstantial at most. He could have lost the jewelry at any point in time."

"What are we supposed to do until she finds something?" I had no idea how long this Josie woman would take to get the evidence they needed to bring O'Reilly to justice.

Connor glared coolly at me. I squirmed under his powerful stare. Good grief, this guy scared me a little.

"Josie is a genius. It shouldn't take her long. Right now, this is her top priority. Until she finds it though, you're going to stay here with Webber and try to stay alive."

Well, gee, that sounded easy enough. So, pretty much, I was supposed to sit around and hope someone didn't kill me. This Connor guy didn't sound too sympathetic.

He turned and directed his next words to Daniel. "Webber, I've got Miles here in charge of security. You'll have a full detail until we can get O'Reilly. Miles will run surveillance during the day and two of my best men will split the evenings. It's your choice, but I wouldn't mention any of this to anyone in your department. We know for a fact that O'Reilly has several cops on his payroll. I believe he's involved in the cover ups we discovered in that last case."

All four of them exchanged a look I couldn't interpret, but clearly some type of communication passed between them. I was curious, but didn't want to ask if front of them all. I'd wait and speak to Daniel after they all left. A ping came from Josie's computer.

"There it is. Damn, that was even faster than I expected. There is a hefty price on your head, Webber. I'm doing what I can to trace everything on O'Reilly, but it's going to take some time, even with my skills."

"Just do what you can, Josie. In the meantime, Miles will be here as a safeguard."

Josie shut down her laptop and pulled Miles aside. They spoke in hushed tones in the kitchen, and it was clear they were saying goodbye. I averted my eyes when they embraced and shared a kiss. Then, she and Connor left, leaving Miles behind.

"I'm gonna head outside and scope out the surroundings. Put up some surveillance equipment that Josie can hack into and keep an eye on things from her end. I'll be outside if you need me."

Miles left Daniel and me alone as he picked up his duffel bag and went outside, closing the door softly behind him.

"Wow, your friends are a little intense. Where did you meet them?"

Daniel squirmed a little as though uncomfortable. He cleared his throat and gave a small cough. "I briefly met Black during a few cases I'd worked that he was involved with on the periphery. But, I also worked a case that involved Black's wife. Although, she wasn't his wife at the time."

Something in his tone had me studying him a little closer. I couldn't be sure, but it almost sounded like chagrin. "It sounds like there's a story there."

I paused to see if he'd fill in the question I'd left hanging.

"It's nothing really."

I should have let it go at that, but for some reason, I just kept pushing. "It doesn't sound like nothing."

Daniel sighed in defeat. "I had a slight interest in his wife, and it led me to briefly forgetting about the case to focus more on fucking with Black. We're not on the best of terms on good days. His wife, who, like I said, wasn't his wife at the time, along with her biological son were kidnapped and almost killed. And it was my fault."

I absorbed his words and irrational jealousy flowed through me. For the briefest moment, I hated this unknown woman because she'd captured Daniel's interest. It didn't matter if she'd returned his regard or not. It didn't even matter that it had happened long before he'd ever met me.

"Hey," Daniel spoke softly as he reached for my hands that I now noticed were clenched in fists at my side. "I'm sorry."

Puzzled, I wasn't sure what he meant. "For what?"

"For lying to you. For telling you that I would bring you nothing but trouble. I've fucked up so much lately, and I don't want to let you down."

My grip tightened on his hands, and I stared up in awe at this flawed man. "Daniel, there is no way you could let me down. I love you. That's why I was so upset this morning. I know I didn't come out and say it, but I do. I love everything about you. Your protectiveness. Your loyalty. The way you make me feel as though I'm the only woman for you."

Our eyes remained on each other, love flowing between us. I knew Daniel loved me. It was in his every touch, even from that first kiss the night Emmett was killed. His need to push me away because he didn't think he was good enough for me spoke of his love.

Daniel reached up, swept my hair away from my face, and cupped my cheek in his large but gentle hands. He rubbed his thumbs across my cheekbones as he bent to place a kiss on my parted lips, and although he didn't say the words back to me, he put every ounce of his feelings into it.

We broke apart; this time, hand in hand, I led Daniel down the hall to his room. After closing and locking the door, I slowly undressed him as he stood there, still as a statue. His body was perfection, and I couldn't help but dip my head and suck the barbell in my mouth, my tongue flicking over it. I'd never really thought about how sexy a man with a pierced nipple would be, but for some reason, it fit Daniel. It and his tattoos only accentuated his beauty.

I wanted him inside me more than I'd ever wanted anything else in my life. Feeling playful, I gave Daniel a soft push, and he plopped down on the edge of the bed. He leaned back on his elbows, his hooded eyes deceptively casual, observing me as I gave a slow tease while I got rid of my own clothes. Pride filled me as his arousal grew at the sight of more exposed skin.

He took a shuddering breath as I peeled the last layer of clothing off to finally reveal my nudity. The minute I shucked my underwear, I didn't hesitate climbing onto his lap, wrapping my arms around his neck, draping myself over him as I began rubbing myself against his erect cock.

"I want to feel everything this time," I said as I stared into his eyes.

His widened in surprise as my words sunk in. "Are you sure?"

I nodded as I pushed my hair over one shoulder, pressed my breasts against his chest, and leaned into him. I initiated the kiss, using my slight leverage over him to control it. A boldness I forgot I had came over me. I kept my hands braced on his shoulders as I ground my pussy against him. I was already wet when we'd entered the room, but my juices flowed out of me as my arousal ratcheted up a few degrees now that we were skin to skin.

I lifted up slightly, and reaching behind me, I clasped his throbbing cock in my hand and guided him to my pussy. Gently lowering myself, I closed my eyes as he filled me to overflowing.

Slowly at first, I began to move up and down, controlling the pace. Daniel's hands gripped my hips tightly, and he groaned in arousal. I kept a slow rhythm, but soon it wasn't enough for either of us. My movements quickened, and my head fell back with every pounding push of his cock inside me. Daniel's grip tightened on my hips, and I could feel him losing his tightly wound control.

Daniel's head dipped, and he took my ruched nipple in his mouth, laving the bud with his tongue, sending another spike of need deep into my core. My inner muscles clenched on his length, causing a groan to vibrate from his chest. A hand traced a path from my hip toward my center, and I gasped as Daniel's finger added to the sensation of pleasure as he flicked it against my clit.

He began drawing slow circles around it, the pressure increasing with each stroke.

Between the finger at my nub and the wet heat of Daniel's mouth surrounding my breast, it suddenly became too much, and the tightly coiled tension that had been building inside me exploded. My release hit, and I ground my pelvis against his while stars exploded behind my eyes. I screamed out Daniel's name as I felt his length tighten, and then he was right behind me, his seed coating me inside. Tiny tremors tickled my spine as my body sagged against Daniel's chest.

Our heavy breathing sounded loud in the otherwise quiet room. Sweat beaded on my forehead and at the nape of my neck. I remained plastered against Daniel, his hands wrapped around my waist, our hearts beating in time with the other, and a feeling of tenderness and love washed over me.

Slowly, I pulled away and could feel Daniel's seed in me. I collapsed in an exhausted heap on the bed next to him, but moved over when he gave me a little nudge so he could lay beside me. I cuddled up to him as he wrapped his strong, loving arms around me. A woman could get used to this.

CHAPTER 17

"I LOVE YOU." The words escaped before I could stop them. But now that they'd taken root, there was no going back. Katie was it for me. She was the woman I wanted to spend the rest of my mornings waking up to. Her face was the last thing I wanted to see before I went to sleep. I had no idea if I was ever going to be good enough for her, but she made me want to be a better person.

Her beautiful ice blue eyes met mine, and a soft smile formed on her lips. "I'm glad you finally admitted it. I love you too, Daniel. Whatever happens, we're in this together. I have faith in your friends and in you. O'Reilly is going down, one way or another. I know it."

"Connor and his team are the best at what they do. Impressive doesn't even begin to describe Josie's skills with the computer. If anyone can find the information to bring down O'Reilly, it's her. In the meantime, it's killing me to leave you alone, even with the guards that Black has assigned, but I have to head into work soon. I also need to check in with some of my friends at the precinct and see what they can give me on O'Reilly."

Katie nodded in understanding, her brown hair dancing against the pillow. My pillow. The place where she belonged. I untangled our limbs and rose from the bed.

"I need to take a quick shower."

"Go ahead, I'm going to head into the kitchen and order food in. Is there anything special you'd like?"

"Don't worry about me; I'll grab a quick bite on the way in."

She looked like she wanted to say something, but she turned and headed out of the room. Hurriedly, I jumped in the shower. I had just finished drying off when Katie came back into the bedroom carrying a cup of coffee.

"Here, at least drink this. You didn't get much sleep last night, and I don't want you falling asleep at work. I wasn't sure if you took anything in it."

She handed me the steaming brew, and I took a cautious sip. Black and delicious. Just the way I liked it. "It's perfect. Thank you."

I quickly got dressed, my cock in a semi-hard state as Katie's eyes roamed over my body while I put on my clothes. She was making it extremely difficult for me to want to leave the house.

We walked hand in hand out to the living room. Katie made herself comfortable on the couch as she thumbed through various takeout menus I had. I stepped outside to find Miles after he'd made himself scarce earlier. Once I located him, I let him know to call me for anything, no matter how small. He shooed me off, clucking like a hen. I knew I was worrying for nothing, but I couldn't shut it off. I knew how dangerous O'Reilly was.

I stepped back inside and said my goodbyes. "Miles will be here for the rest of the night. He'll introduce you to his replacement whenever he gets here. Trust them. If they think something is wrong, listen to them. Understand?"

"Yes, sir." Katie gave me a smart salute.

"I'm serious."

She sobered at my tone. "Daniel, I understand. I'll trust them because you do."

My hands cradled her head as I reached down to taste her lips. Our lips tangled, and I enjoyed her flavor longer than I should have. Reluctantly, I pulled away and forced myself to walk out the door.

FOR FOUR DAYS we followed the same routine. Each night, when I got home, no matter that it was practically early morning, Katie and I made love. We slept for a few hours here and there. Then, in the afternoon, I went back to work. I'd spoken to some of the guys, but none of them had been able to find any kind of evidence on O'Reilly either. The man was excellent at making things—and people—disappear. There had been multiple charges brought up against him, from assault and battery to murder, but none of the charges had ever stuck.

Miles and the other two guards, who I only knew as Fredericks and Jones, continued to switch shifts and watch the house. Josie had reported that no unusual activity had been seen from the surveillance equipment Miles had installed that first day. She did say she was close to pinning some things on O'Reilly. In the meantime, nothing had changed. No attempts had been made on our lives. No disruptions whatsoever. I knew O'Reilly wanted us to think he'd given up so we'd let our guard down, become complacent, but I knew that wasn't the case. We'd royally pissed him off, and he wasn't going to forget or forgive that.

It was early morning on the fifth day that it finally happened. As much as we thought we were ready, we weren't. It was the wee hours of the morning, and Jones had just taken over Fredericks shift. It was my day off so Katie and I were sleeping. I woke suddenly as though my subconscious knew something big was about to go down. I lay there, straining to hear any unusual sounds. It was too quiet. My head turned to look at the clock on my nightstand, but everything was black. The power was out. Or had been cut. I reached into the drawer next to me and pulled out my gun. I slipped out of bed, careful not to disturb Katie.

Quietly, I made my way down the hall on full alert. I'd just reached the end, where it opened into the living room, when I heard a groan of pain. In the moonlight, I spotted Jones on the floor in the kitchen. I crouched down next to him, still keeping my senses open to my surroundings. That's when I noticed the blood pooling beneath him. He'd been bashed over the head with a blunt object and was just coming to.

A soft click sounded behind me. "Put your gun on the floor and slide it across the floor. Then, take a step back and put your hands in the air, Detective."

Shit. I did as I was told. When I stood and moved away from the body, a light clicked on. In the living room, sitting on my couch, looking far too relaxed, was Francis O'Reilly. Standing next to him stood two of his guards. I'd learned through Josie that their names were Tony and Ricco. Ricco's most distinguishing feature was the large scar across his face. Otherwise, he looked like your typical muscle for hire. Josie said he was brutal and relished making people hurt. He also had no qualms about killing when asked. Tony, on the other hand was an enigma. Josie couldn't find anything on him. It was as though he didn't exist.

"You didn't think I was going to forget you owe me, did you?" O'Reilly drawled, every word dripping with hatred.

"Honestly, I expected you here a lot sooner. You're slipping."

"You and your girlfriend have the same smart mouth, I see. You realize we have a problem, right?"

"Get out of my house, and we'll have less of a problem."

Tony chuckled, but stifled it when O'Reilly shot a glare at him. Clearly, someone didn't appreciate my sense of humor. I had to keep O'Reilly talking until the cavalry arrived. I knew by now that Connor was on his way. It was just a matter of staying alive until he got here. Even now, it pissed me off that Black was, more than likely, going to have to rescue me. This was going to be one more thing for him to bust my balls about. Internally, I groaned. But, I continued to try and play it cool.

"You've gotten away with Jackson's murder. How are you going to explain away three more deaths?" I asked, continuing to stall the inevitable.

O'Reilly settled himself even deeper into the couch. "Who says I need to explain anything? Nobody will connect me to your death. I've gotten away with far more crimes. Adding a few more to my total won't make much difference."

"You yourself mentioned how industrious my friends are. I can guarantee they're going to know you're behind this."

"I'm not too worried about your friends. I have my own extremely powerful allies."

I heard a soft gasp behind me and knew our time was up. Katie stood at the entrance of the living room, sleep tousled hair falling over a single shoulder. I had the urge to run over and wrap my arms around her and tell her that nothing would harm her.

"Ah, so glad the lovely Ms. Marsh could finally join

us. Ricco, why don't you escort the lady over to the chair over there? It's important for her to have a front row seat."

My fists clenched in anger as I watched, helplessly, as O'Reilly's man tried to take Katie's arm. I silently applauded her, yet also cringed, when she jerked her arm away from the man and proudly walked to the chair of her own accord. I was proud of her pluck, even though I wanted to warn her to be careful. The slightest move could push O'Reilly's patience past his breaking point. Eventually, he'd get there, but right now it looked like he wanted to play games.

Katie took her seat, but remained tense. Ricco remained standing next to her, although I saw Tony move a little closer to them, a flash of some unreadable emotion gracing his face before it became blank again. My gaze moved from them back to O'Reilly, who had begun to rise from his position on the couch. My eyes followed his as he slowly wandered around the room, studying everything including pictures I had hung on the wall or placed on various surfaces.

"You have a beautiful family, Detective. Your sisters are gorgeous. Your mom as well."

I knew he was taunting me, but I still rose to his bait.

"Stay the fuck away from my family."

He turned from his spot near the fireplace and addressed me. "You're not really in a position to make demands. So, here's the deal. Your Ms. Marsh signs over her entire inheritance to me and your family is safe."

"I already told you the money was yours," Katie cried out from the other side of the room.

"Oh, yes, I know. But, I haven't finished my bargaining, yet. Also, Detective, you will turn over everything you think you have on me. Everything."

"You're going to kill us anyway. Why should I give you what you want? Either way, we're dead."

O'Reilly nodded at Ricco who, before I could blink, grabbed Katie's hair, yanked her head back, and placed the knife I hadn't seen him pull out at her throat. She screamed in pain as a small drop of blood trickled down her neck.

"Uh uh uh," O'Reilly barked as I made to lunge in their direction. I stopped short at his words. "I wouldn't do that if I were you."

Suddenly, everything happened at once. The front door burst open, and Connor and Miles barreled through, guns drawn, and Tony dove for Ricco, ripping the knife away from Katie's neck just as I reached her. I pulled her into my arms, her sobs echoing in my ears.

I heard Connor's barked order of "put the gun down", then several gunshots had my attention on the other side of the room where O'Reilly now lay on the ground, writhing in pain, a small gun at his side. Connor stepped over to him and, using a rag from his pocket to avoid fingerprints, picked up the pistol and laid it on the mantel. Seeing that O'Reilly was no longer a threat, I focused on Katie. I pulled slightly away from her as my eyes scanned her body, taking note of the trickle of blood still lightly falling from the shallow cut on her neck. It didn't look deep, but I still wanted to kill the man who put it there.

A scuffle next to us had me pushing Katie behind me, and I saw Tony and Ricco wrestling on the floor for control of the knife. Back and forth they went, until finally, Ricco's scream of agony echoed in the air as Tony snapped his wrist, the knife falling uselessly to the floor. Tony kicked it across the room and out of reach before turning to face us.

"My name is Anthony Rodriguez, and I'm an undercover D.E.A. agent."

Slowly, he reached one hand into his back pocket and pulled out a wallet before tossing it into my outstretched hand. I stared down at the picture I.D. for a moment before throwing it over to Connor.

"Tell her to contact Director Timothy Shepherd. He'll verify everything I'm telling you. I've been working undercover for over three years gathering intel to bring O'Reilly's racketeering organization down. We discovered over a year ago that he's been dabbling in arms dealing with the Russians, and we've been building a case to connect him to Vladamir Dragomirov in an attempt to take Drago down."

My gaze shot to Black and Standish at the Russian's name. It was a name we were all highly familiar with. This case had just taken another dangerous turn.

"Josie, I need you to confirm that an Anthony Rodriguez is D.E.A. " Connor spoke through his Bluetooth before lobbing the wallet back to Rodriguez who returned it to his pocket.

"You fucking traitor."

My head snapped back to O'Reilly, whom I'd completely forgotten about. While our focus had been elsewhere, he'd risen from the floor and had a gun pointed at Rodriguez.

Connor and Miles quickly turned and directed their guns at the threat. "Don't do it, O'Reilly."

His entire focus was on the man across the room. "I trusted you, and this is how you repay me? You were part of my family. How dare you come to my house and betray us like this."

"Put the gun down, Francis," Rodriguez tried coaxing. "You know there's only one way this is going to go down. You're going to prison, O'Reilly."

"The hell I am. I'll die first." His finger twitched and another round of gunshots sounded as I dragged Katie to the floor, covering her body with mine. When the smoke cleared, O'Reilly was back on the ground, but this time, I knew he wasn't getting back up. I looked around and saw that somehow a gun had appeared in Rodriguez's hand. I had no idea who truly fired the kill shot, but my guess was from the man in front of me.

I pulled Katie back up from the ground and pulled her to me.

"It's over, love."

"God, Daniel, I was so scared. But, I knew you wouldn't let anything happen to me."

"I love you so much, Katherine Marsh."

"I love you too, Daniel."

While I held her, Connor, Miles, and Rodriguez all made various phone calls. Shortly after, sirens could be heard getting closer. Soon, the house was filled with D.E.A. and paramedics who were treating Ricco. They put him on a stretcher and wheeled him out to an ambulance. An agent hopped up into the back of the vehicle and, after closing the back doors, the truck drove off. O'Reilly's body was bagged and taken to the coroner's office.

During the entire time, I refused to release my hold on Katie. She was in my arms, and I was never letting her go after this.

EPILOGUE

It was hard to believe that it had been over two months since everything went down. I still woke with the occasional nightmare, but Daniel was there to wrap me in his arms and comfort me as the tears came. I'd moved into his house, and we were both adjusting. A huge shake up happened at City Hall a couple weeks after O'Reilly's death. Both the Mayor of Pinegrove and the Chief of Police were finally indicted on charges after Black and his team at Blacklight Securities uncovered more incriminating evidence against them during their investigation into Francis O'Reilly. I'd had no idea that they'd already been under investigation for other crimes until Daniel told me.

Because of the corruption in the system, Daniel was considering retiring from the force and actually going to work with Connor at Blacklight. I could tell it surprised both of them when Connor offered Daniel a position if he wanted it. I knew they would always butt heads, but Daniel was tired of the bureaucracy. He would also have a lot more freedom and more resources at his disposal to truly help people, which was the whole reason he'd wanted to become a police officer in the first place. We had talked about it, but he hadn't made a final decision, although I knew he was headed that way. Regardless of what decision he made, I would fully support him. We both could tell though that his heart was no longer in it.

I'd also finally received the pay out from Emmett's life insurance policy. It took me the longest time to figure out what I was going to do with both the money and La Scala. I knew it had been Emmett's dream to turn the restaurant into something big. But, as I came to discover, it hadn't been my dream. I found a buyer and ended up selling it for a small loss. It hurt for a while that I'd had to give it up, but I knew it was for the best. I used a portion of the money after deciding I wanted to go back to college for something *I* wanted to do.

I'd told Daniel I'd always wanted to be a social worker who helped kids like me. Kids whose parents weren't there for them the way mine hadn't been there for me. So, I enrolled in the local community college and started working toward my degree in social work.

The rest of the money I invested for our future. Or rather, the future of our children. Something I had never considered until a couple weeks ago when I peed on that little stick and two blue lines showed up. I hadn't told Daniel yet, but I knew I needed to soon. Neither of us had discussed marriage or kids, and I was nervous as all get out. I wanted nothing more than to have children with Daniel, but I didn't know how to approach it with him.

"How's my sexy little mama doing today?" I snuggled back into a warm chest as strong arms wrapped around me, pulling me tightly against the hard body behind me. I turned my head to meet Daniel's kiss. Then it hit me what he'd said, and I quickly turned to face him.

"How did you know?" I couldn't hide my shock.

"Know what?"

"That I was pregnant."

He laughed a little as his hands roamed over my body. "Sweetheart, I know your body better than I know my own. Your boobs are slightly bigger, and you've been eating a lot more than you usually do." At that, I lightly smacked him on the arm. I couldn't help it I had a healthy appetite.

"Besides," he continued, "we've been having unprotected sex since the beginning, and don't think I haven't failed to notice that the entire time you've been living here, not once have you had your period. Plus, I found the pregnancy test you tried so hard to hide. I *am* a detective, you know."

Sudden shyness overcame me, and I couldn't look at him. Strong fingers hooked under my chin and lifted my head up so I was forced to meet his eyes.

"What's wrong? Are you not happy about the baby?"

I wanted to smack myself when I heard the nervousness in his voice. It struck me that he was afraid this wasn't what I wanted.

"Oh, Daniel. I've never been happier. You're going to be an amazing father. I just wasn't sure how you felt about it. We never really talked about long term, and we definitely didn't talk about kids. I was worried about telling you."

Daniel led me over the couch and dragged me onto his lap as he sat down. He caressed my face, pushing my hair out of my eyes. He stared so intently at me that I forced myself not to fidget.

"I don't ever want you to have to worry about talking to me. About anything. I love you, Katherine. I'm in this for the long haul, whatever that entails. Marriage, kids, Little League. All of it. I want it, and I want it with you. Always."

I sighed in contentment that I'd finally found my happy place, in Daniel's arms.

Thank you for reading **PROTECT**. I hope you enjoyed it. I'd greatly appreciate a review on the platform of your choice. Reviews are so important!

Find out what ever happened with Josie's sister, Phebe, in BETRAYAL.

BETRAYAL

Death.

Blessed release.

Neither would be coming for me no matter how much I wished otherwise.

Instead, I was stuck living in this hell I now called life. A sob disguised as a laugh escaped before I could stop it, and the echo of the sound bouncing off the walls mocked me. I thought I was going mad, and to be honest, I welcomed the madness. Perhaps if I were mad, I could forget what was happening to me. Sadly, I knew no such thing would happen.

No matter what they did to me, my mind remained intact.

Luck never came to people like me.

I closed my eyes and pictured sunlight. I thought about the sun and the way the rays of light would catch on a raindrop and produce the brilliant colors of the rainbow. The way it sparkled like diamonds on glistening, white snow. I could almost swear my body heated imperceptibly with the thought of the sun shining down on it. Mentally I absorbed the heat and forced the chills to escape my cold, half-naked form lying on the even colder floor.

A countless number of days had passed, how many I couldn't tell. I'd lost track, and soon they ran together in nothing but one endless night. One that was nightmare filled.

A shiver racked my body and my mind drifted back to the faux sunshine coming through the non-existent window in my cell wall. And it *was* a cell. Gray stone walls surrounded me on three sides, and I refused to open my eyes to the steel bars in front of me. I didn't need to open them to know they were there. I received nearly daily reminders when my captors led me through them to whatever fate awaited me on the other side.

A muffled sound came from far away, but I ignored it. My punishment would come soon enough. The sound grew louder, but I blocked the noise out. Sunshine was my only friend in this bleak existence I now found myself in. I heard a crash outside the entrance to the room my cell was housed in. Instinctively, I flinched when the door slammed open. I didn't move again. Not that it would have mattered. I would have made myself smaller, and less conspicuous, if I thought it would make a difference. I remained curled on my side, my knees tucked to my chest. This was it. My training was over. I'd finally been broken, and he was here to claim his prize.

"Phebe? Phebe Lawson?"

Well, shit. I guess wishes do come true. My mind had finally snapped.

Knowing I wouldn't see anything, I forced my eyes to open and raised my head, because I thought my eyes were deceiving me.

Blink. Blink.

A hazy outline of a man, with what appeared to be a gun drawn, stood silhouetted in the doorway. Finally, death had come to take me away. A sweet relief coursed through me, and my head sagged back down to the floor.

"She's in here! She's alive." The booming voice sounded too loud in my ears.

Metal against metal scraped my eardrums as a key was thrust into the lock of my cell door. It clanged against the wall as it was hastily tore open. Tentative footsteps moved closer, and I waited for the gunshot. I hoped he made it quick. However, instead of the pain of a bullet, the bittersweet pain of a soft touch floated across my hair, gently moving it out of my face.

"Phebe." The deep male voice came from directly above me. Why was he torturing me? Just do it and get it over with. Against my will, a tear spilled from behind my closed eyes. A thumb ghosted across my cheek taking the moisture with it, causing another involuntary flinch.

"Phebe, my name is Daniel Webber. I'm with the Pinegrove Police. I'm here to take you home."

~

My eyes scanned the room Detective Webber had dropped me off in before he'd headed back out to find someone named Connor. I was thankful the couch was positioned so my back was to the wall. No one could sneak up on me then. The ticking clock reminded me that it was well past dark, and I hadn't eaten for awhile. My empty, growling stomach was also a reminder, but I tended to ignore that. No sense wishing for food when it only appeared when he was feeling generous.

Webber had grabbed his overcoat from the back of his vehicle, and I'd shrugged into it to cover my near nakedness when I'd left my cold, dank cell. He'd taken me to the police station where I'd been questioned and promised he would get me a shower and some clothes as soon as he could.

A mixture of dehydration, lack of food, and pure despondency made it difficult to recollect anything. Once I'd given my statement, tonelessly answered all the police's invasive questions, and refused to go to the hospital, Webber escorted me outside. He asked if I had any place to go, and when I'd shaken my head, he shot me a look of pity and told me he'd take me some place safe.

Supposedly, this office was my safe place. It was expensively decorated without being flashy. The wet bar was stocked as well as any club I'd been to. The dark leather couch and office chair smelled wonderful, almost new. There was even a hint of some fancy men's cologne on the air. My eyes closed briefly as I deeply inhaled all the scents. Anything to cleanse the stink of my prison from my nostrils. The smells I was finally free from in that hell hole. A barely discernible noise had my eyes snapping open.

When the door slowly opened, I realized the noise had been a light knock. Webber stepped through first and gave me what I thought was a reassuring look. Walking in behind him was another man. He was massive; built like a brick house with wide, muscular shoulders that tapered to a narrow waist. He had close cut, dark brown hair without a fleck of gray even though he looked close to Kieran's age. His fierce expression had me trembling. Until he smiled. It softened his features and made him marginally less scary looking.

Webber spoke first. "Ms. Lawson, this is Connor Black. This is his office of his company, Blacklight Securities. I know you're probably exhausted, and I know I promised you could get cleaned up, but if you could just give him a little bit of your time, we'd greatly appreciate it."

The only place I could have gone was The Haven, but once Kieran discovered I'd been rescued, that'd be the first place he would look for me. I didn't want to put the women in danger by hiding out there. It was best if I stayed far away from them, from my former life. Which meant, whether I wished to be or not, I was stuck here.

I couldn't hide my bitterness. "Considering I have no where else to go, I guess I have nothing but time to give."

"Ms. Lawson—" Connor, started, as he settled behind his desk. Webber sat in a chair on the opposite side of the room from me. They both seemed to be giving me my space. I was grateful for it. Even if they were here to help me, it made me uneasy being in a room with two men, virtual strangers, although the door had remained open.

"Phebe. My name is Phebe." I interrupted, needing to hear my real name being spoken. I was no longer *malen'kaya igrushka,* or little toy. I was *Phebe*.

"Phebe, then. My employees and I have been diligently working on gathering charges against Mr. Underwood. We have a significant list of crimes, not the least of which is ties to a Russian sex-trafficking operation, as evidenced by where we discovered you. Sadly, you weren't the only woman being held captive, although you were one of the luckier ones. I know you spoke to the police about what happened to you, but there is only so much the police can do. They have hundreds of cases that cross their desk every day. There is also some internal shit going down that is going to make prosecuting this case low importance. You, however, are our number one priority. Righting the wrongs against you is our main objective."

His words sounded foreign to me. *Luckier ones? Did he*

think I hadn't heard the screams of the other women? I was a mere ghost of my former self. How in God's name was I a lucky one? Why did these people care about what happened to me?

"You're lucky because you're not addicted to heroine and other drugs like some of the women that were found. You're lucky because you're alive. And we care, because you're one of us."

I hadn't realized I asked the questions out loud, but now I was even more confused.

"What do you mean I'm one of you?"

The detective and Mr. Black exchanged a questioning glance. It was as though an entire conversation took place between them. Finally, Connor spoke up.

"Do you know who your father was, Phebe?"

I shook my head in puzzlement, wondering what he had to do with anything. "I know of him, but he isn't a part of my life. Wait, what do you mean was?"

"I'm afraid he's dead." His words held a hint of satisfaction.

"Dead?" I echoed.

"There really isn't any easy way to break this to you other than to just spit it out. Mr. Underwood worked for your father. Your father was the main reason we even knew of your existence." Connor's gaze was filled with pity as he continued destroying me without even realizing it. "Before he died, he confessed to what had become of you to his daughter."

He paused, letting his words sink in. When they

finally did, tears I didn't even know I had left fell from my eyes.

Kieran worked for my father?

After all these years, how could I have not known that? I'd always assumed Kieran was his own boss. Was that why he'd asked me out all those years ago? Why he threatened me if I ever left? Suddenly, I questioned everything about my former life.

And now I'd learned something else.

"I have a sister?" I asked, wiping away the tears.

"Well, a half-sister if you want to get technical. She works for me as a computer analyst. Josephine also has a few extra skill sets that allowed her to track you down. She's the one who sent Webber to your location."

My muddled brain was having trouble processing everything. Spots danced in my eyes and a buzzing sounded in my ears before everything started to go black.

"Ms. Lawson. Phebe!" My eyes focused and I snapped to attention. Webber squatted at my feet, but didn't attempt to touch me in any way.

"Sorry," my voice came out shaky. "I haven't eaten in a while. Do you mind if I have something to drink?"

The detective's horrified expression would have normally been comical if I still wasn't feeling woozy.

"Jesus, I wasn't even thinking." He stood and grabbed a bottle of water from the bar fridge. He also handed me some type of protein bar Connor had tossed him from his desk drawer. A commotion sounded out in the hall.

Connor excused himself and closed the door behind him, effectively locking Webber and me in together. I struggled to breathe a little at the claustrophobic sensation that suddenly engulfed me.

"Phebe. Hey, it's okay. You're safe, remember? No one is going to hurt you here."

I nodded my head in understanding because I knew he expected it.

It took me longer to bring my brain and body up to speed.

Eventually, they both caught up and my breathing slowed to a normal pace. My stomach growled reminding me of my hunger. I took a small bite of the protein bar and chased it with the water. Loud voices, one a female's, could be heard out in the hall. I looked questioningly at Webber. He smiled and nodded as though all was well. The noise quieted out in the hall and a few moments later Connor re-entered the room.

"Are you doing okay?" he asked, concern radiating from him.

"I'm fine now."

He nodded before continuing, gentler this time. "Due to your connection to Josie, you're one of us. We'll do everything we can to make sure Underwood is punished. We're also working with the FBI on locating and prosecuting the man we believe is the head of the trafficking ring. We need your help though. Are you willing to testify against Mr. Underwood regarding his criminal activities as well as anything you might remember about the events leading up to your captivity? And as painful as it may be, we also need you to recall anything you are able to during your time in that cell. Names. Faces. Information regarding their operation they may have let slip in your presence."

Hysterical laughter threatened to explode from me. All I wanted to do was forget the last two months and here these people, these strangers, were asking me to remember? To recall the faces of the men, one man in particular, who took delight in breaking me? To relive every hellish moment I spent in that cell, praying for it all to end? Hadn't I been tortured enough? Apparently not.

They also wanted me as a witness against Kieran's crimes. After all I'd been through, I didn't know if I was ready for that, for any of this. I knew I hated him; had for years. Yet, there was still that part of me that was terrified of him. Of what he'd do to me if I ever spoke out against him. I refused to acknowledge my terror of the Russian. My gaze went back and forth between the two men. Did I dare trust them to keep me safe? My faith in people, men especially, wasn't strong. I'd been let down so many times in my life by people I thought I could trust.

Then, against my will, I thought of *him*. His voice, with its Russian accent, taunting me about about how he'd purchased me like a piece of meat from Kieran. About how I was his.

I remembered, no matter how much I tried to push it out of my head, being powerless. I never wanted to feel that way again. If putting these men away gave me even an ounce of power back, I'd do it.

No woman... no person, should ever be subjected to what I'd gone through. Renewed hatred for him burned through my veins. It sizzled inside my gut and I knew what needed to be done. I had no illusions that it would be easy. My mind wasn't screwed on tight right now. I knew that; recognized it. Fear permeated every pore in my body. Fear my time spent being broken had cultivated. But if I was ever going to survive, I had to do it.

I swallowed hard and nodded. "Yes, I'll do whatever you need me to do." I was resolute in my decision.

By the faint smiles on their faces, both men were pleased with my answer.

Connor spoke again. "Josie worked her ass off to find you and to put together a case against Underwood. She's desperate to meet you. I wasn't sure if you were ready or not so I made her stay in her office. Are you up to seeing her?"

So, from what Connor'd said, this Josie was my sister. A sister I never even knew I had. As unfair as it was, I couldn't help the bitterness that spread through me. If Josie was as good with computers as Connor had alluded to, why hadn't she tracked me down sooner? Maybe this —brokenness— wouldn't have happened to me. No, I couldn't do it. Not right now. Hateful thoughts ran through my head. Thoughts I had no control over.

"No, I don't want to see her."

Connor nodded as though expecting my answer. "I'll

let her know. She won't be happy, but she'll respect your decision. If you change your mind, let me know. Now, I know you're exhausted and starving. I'm not going to keep you here any longer. Webber says you don't have anywhere to go. Is that true?"

Ashamed, I could only nod, refusing to make eye contact.

"Webber's going to take you to a safe house. One we use to keep people hidden. No one else stays there so you won't be bothered by anyone. You'll have a crew of men you'll never see securing the house. No one will disturb you, except you'll get an occasional visit from Webber, me, or my wife, Bridget. She'll bring you groceries and some new clothes in the morning. You'll find a few t-shirts and sweatpants in the dresser. There's also enough food in the house to last you until then. In the next week, you'll be meeting the prosecuting attorney in the case. He's a friend so you don't have to worry about him. Now, do you have any questions?"

"No." There wasn't much more to say at the moment. I was only glad they didn't ask me about the last few months yet. About my captor. My destroyer.

Connor made his way to the door, but before he opened it, he turned slightly to peer at me over his shoulder. "They won't get away with what they did to you. Whether it be in a court of law or not, I swear to you, neither of them will get away with it."

Without waiting for a response, he left the room, his words echoing inside my head.

"Are you ready to go?" Webber's voice shook me out of my frozen state.

"I'm ready." No more untrue words had ever been spoken. I wasn't ready for any of this. Regardless of what I'd agreed to, I didn't think I'd ever be ready.

Get your copy of BETRAYAL today!

Doms of Club Eden
Submission
Desire
Redemption
Protect
Betrayal
Mistletoe
Absolution
Merry Eden

To Love and Protect
In Too Deep
Striking Distance
Atonement
Bullet Proof
For Always
Point Blank
Saving Evie

Brooklyn Kings
The Devil I Don't Know
The Enemy in My Bed
The Beast I Can't Tame
Irish Devil
Irish Rogue
Irish Charmer
Irish Rebel

Dublin Kings
Cian

Other Books
Love Notes: A Dark Romance
SEALs in Love
Say Yes
Black Light: Possession

ABOUT THE AUTHOR

LK Shaw is the bestselling author of sexy, sinful suspense. She resides in South Carolina. She is a dog mom and self proclaimed chocolate lover, world traveler, and perpetual procrastinator. An avid reader since childhood, she became hooked on historical romance novels in high school. She now reads, and loves, all romance sub-genres. Her books feature sexy, protective heroes and the strong women they love.

Be sure to sign up for her newsletter and download your FREE ebook!

https://bit.ly/LKShawNewsletter

Printed in Great Britain
by Amazon